A boy was walking along the path toward me. He was tall and slim, with dark wavy hair, and his arm circled the waist of a pretty girl. It could have been *Ron and me. I took off at a run and ran into a fence. Just beyond the barrier was the putting green of the golf course. Four men were silhouetted against the darkening sky. Suddenly a huge sprinkler switched on. But the men went right on putting, even though they were being drenched.*

Golfers are crazy, I decided. They don't know when they're wet. They don't know when to quit. Suddenly, excitement stirred deep within me. I wanted to be crazy, too.

Dear Reader,

At Silhouette we publish books with you in mind. We're pleased to announce the creation of Silhouette First Love, a new line of contemporary romances written by the finest young-adult writers as well as outstanding new authors in this field.

Silhouette First Love captures many of the same elements enjoyed by Silhouette Romance readers—love stories, happy endings and the same attention to detail and description. But First Love features young heroines and heroes in contemporary and recognizable situations.

You play an important part in our future plans for First Love. We welcome any suggestions or comments on our books and I invite you to write to us at the address below.

Karen Solem
Editor-in-Chief
Silhouette Books
P.O. Box 769
New York, N.Y. 10019

GIRL IN
THE ROUGH
Josephine Wunsch

First Love from Silhouette

Published by Silhouette Books New York

America's Publisher of Contemporary Romance

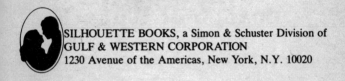SILHOUETTE BOOKS, a Simon & Schuster Division of
GULF & WESTERN CORPORATION
1230 Avenue of the Americas, New York, N.Y. 10020

ISBN: 0-671-53302-9

First Silhouette Books printing October, 1981

10 9 8 7 6 5 4 3 2 1

GIRL IN
THE ROUGH

1

Mimi's little ways were getting to me.

Mom called it the Lottery of Genes and said that my year-younger sister could no more control the heredity that made her petite and pretty like our Louisville grandmother than I could help taking after Dad's side of the family—big boned and brainy.

Maybe I can't help what I am, but something has to be done. What's been happening around here is too much. All afternoon the phone's been ringing for Mimi—girlfriends and boyfriends and some nut who snorted in heavy gasps and then hung up.

Usually I'm not in on the zoo. When I come

home, I shut myself in my room and study. But today I was expecting a call of my own. Ron. Now, prowling restlessly from the living room into the dining alcove, I wondered how the debate was going, wondered if the words I wrote suited his special style.

I flung open the patio door and took a deep breath of the sweet spring air. Was the garden more beautiful this year or was I seeing it through Ron's poetic eye? The forsythia was no longer a bush of bare branches. It was a gushing fountain splashing yellow blossoms on the back fence. The magnolia spilled shell-pink tears on a green carpet. Funny what Ron could do to me. If he's happy, I'm happy. If he's sad, I'm sunk.

I'm such a klutz, I hadn't expected anyone as gorgeous as Ron to notice me. We met at the library and, in time, planned meetings at the back table. We sat side by side, so when he got hung up on his homework, I was right there to help him. Sometimes we held hands under the table, and if luck was with us we exchanged quick kisses in the back stacks.

I had no intention of bringing him home—not with schemy-Mimi in the picture—but yesterday afternoon he just showed up.

"Help, Kate!" He grasped both my hands and his luminous eyes pleaded with me. "Everything's riding on my speech tomorrow and I'm stymied."

I rushed him into the den and closed the door, shutting Mimi out.

It was Mom who found us and invited Ron to stay for dinner.

We worked hard and late. Now I began to jitter. The big debate should be over by now.

At last, the shrilling of the phone jived with the bonging of the hall clock.

Mimi leaned over the banister, blond hair swinging. "I'll get it, Kate."

"No. This one's for me."

A brow arched. "But who would call you?"

"For me," I said, and pushed shut the door of the TV room with the toe of my sneaker. I reached for the receiver, my voice edgy with excitement. "How did it go, Ron?"

"Hey, Kate!" A familiar chuckle. "How did you guess?"

"It had to be you." I pictured the warm dark eyes, the quick grin. "You said you'd phone as soon as the debate was over. Five o'clock." I paused. "Out with it. Did you win?"

"But barely. A close decision. The work you

did on my speech last night kicked it over, I'm sure."

I leaned back, stretching the full length of the couch, my head curved into the pillow, my legs dangling over the end.

"Oh, it's one thing to make a point on paper, but it's something else to stand up and convince all those judges."

"You're my silent partner, Kate."

Partner. I liked that. One thing about Ron. He was confident (some people called him cocky), but he always let me know how much he appreciated any little thing I did for him.

"Now about that super supper," Ron said. "Your father kept loading my plate with chow and I fear I shortchanged the rest of you."

Actually I hadn't noticed. I'd been concentrating too hard on his speech, trying to shut out Mimi's mindless chatter, so that I could come up with a conclusion that had clout.

"Now that you know what a good cook Mom is," I said, "try us again."

"Will do," Ron said, and without even a pause added, "Let me have a word with that kid sister."

I pushed the receiver away from my ear, holding it at arm's length, a deadly snake ready to strike. Ron's voice came in distinctly. "Hullo, hullo, are you there?"

In that moment I knew I was a loser again.

"Hang on." I ground the words out. I called upstairs. "Mimi! The phone's for you."

I went to my room and closed the door. I sat at my desk and stared at Samson and Delilah streaking in gold circles around the fish bowl. Mimi bounded in.

"Don't you ever knock?" I said.

"Ron wants me to go with him to the June Jamboree. Can you imagine old North High having the luck to get the Funky Five?"

"So—"

Mimi teetered on the edge of the bed. She looked young and vulnerable with her long hair parted in the middle and held by blue ribbons that matched her eyes. An Alice-in-Wonderland figure, but far too aware to fall down a rabbit hole.

"I told Ron I'd call back," she said. "If Ron's someone you go for"—she spread her dainty fingers and the charms on her bracelet jangled—"I'll tell him to forget it."

"Tell him any old thing. I don't care."

"Don't be that way," Mimi said. "Let's level with each other. I promise I won't ever make a

play for someone you like, and if there's someone I think is really neat, I hope you won't cut
me out."

"Me?" I laughed loudly. Every boy I'd ever
looked at, Mimi had snapped up. Then, like fish
too small to keep, she'd tossed him back. Only
this time it was different. I cared about Ron.

Mimi leaned closer, bringing an aura of perfume, body lotions, bath oils. Everything so
perfect—the tiny pearl teeth, the tip-tilted nose,
the dark lashes and brows against the fair skin,
the little earlobes.

"How is that pretty daughter of yours?" The
question everyone asked Mother.

"Which one?" Mom always said.

But even at an early age I knew The One.
"Pretty is as pretty does," Mother said, but it
wasn't that way at all. Oh, yes, Mom tried to be
proud of me. I was on the Honor Roll and she
encouraged me. She said I was lucky to be born
now, when there were so many opportunities
for women to succeed in so many exciting fields.
Agreed. And if I made it to the top? Did Ms.
Success have to have a heart of stone?

Mimi's voice, insistent. "You still haven't
answered me, Kate. Is Ron someone special or
just a nobody who keeps bugging you to help

him with his homework because you're so smart?"

"He's a nerd," I said.

Mimi left. Her cologne lingered on. Through glazed eyes I watched Samson and Delilah dart in and out of their rock castle. Oh, to be a fish, coldblooded, without feelings.

2

"What do you think, Kate?" Mimi tucked a silk rose behind her ear.

"I think I'm going to throw up," I said.

Mimi had spent hours dressing for the Jamboree. She had arranged her hair a dozen different ways and had tried on all the jewelry in the house—pearls, seashells, chains.

In the distance, the roar of a car. I held my breath. The car went by. Any minute now Ron would arrive and there I'd be, standing around in jeans watching The Princess descend the stairs. I wanted none of it.

"I'm going out," I announced, and banged the front door.

"Come back before dark," Mother said automatically.

No place to go really. But wasn't any place better than home? The evening was warm with a potpourri of fragrances, mock orange, wisteria, and jasmine scenting the air. Soothing, but I felt all wound up, ready to explode, and I hated myself for letting Mimi and Ron do this to me. I set off down the block, a mishmash of houses, new and old, ranches, neat brick colonials, a contemporary winging out like a butterfly in flight, and, straddling the double lot next door, a Centennial farmhouse surrounded by vegetable and flower gardens.

"How do, Kate." Mr. Dubois looked up from his hoe. He touched his hand to his bald head as if doffing a cap.

I liked Mr. Dubois. He offered bits of philosophy along with his vegetables. On Halloween he gave each kid on the block a pumpkin—"big ones for big kids, little ones for little kids."

Usually I stopped to chat, but now I waved and kept going. Near the corner, two small boys ambushed me.

"Stick 'em up!"

"No games!" I said in my meanest voice. With their curls and pink cheeks, Charles and Cecil looked cherubic, but I knew what monsters they were and refused to baby-sit with them.

Music blasted across the still air. The party at North High had begun. It was hard to believe that North was four blocks away with the brasses beating at my ears.

Unbidden, a picture of a beautiful Kate dancing with a beautiful Ron superimposed itself on my mind. I willed the picture to go away. I turned my back on the school and started to run—faster and faster, until I outdistanced the pursuing notes.

I reached Willow Tree Park surprised that I'd come so far—over two miles from home. Dad always said we were lucky to have a nature spot within walking distance, but who needs it? The last time I'd been here was for a Brownie cookout.

Aimlessly I followed a winding path by picnic tables with white paper cloths and heaps of hot dogs and potato salad and hungry kids lined up along the benches. The tennis courts were jumping too. Couples running and laughing and slamming the ball, sometimes over the net, sometimes into it. I moved along to the baseball diamond, where a Little League game was in progress. I sat down on the bleachers behind home plate, but felt out of it among the cheering parents.

Everybody had a somebody.

I got up and started around the pond in the center of the park. Willow trees clung to the bank, slender leafy branchlets swaying above the murky water. A boy was walking along the path toward me. He was tall, slim, with dark wavy hair, and his arm circled the waist of a pretty girl. It could have been Ron. My scalp began to burn. I took off at a run. I ran right into a fence. I pressed against it, my fingers clutching the mesh.

A golf course, with the putting green just beyond the barrier. I stood there, my breath coming in gasps, and watched. Four men were silhouetted against the darkening sky.

"Your turn." The man standing by the flagstick signaled a golfer across the green.

"See this." With a tap of his putter, the man sent the ball rolling into the tiny cup.

"Yahoo!" The man shouted.

A hiss and a huge sprinkler switched on, showering the putting surface. A fine mist blew my way and I backed off. But the men went right on putting even though they were being drenched.

17

Golfers are crazy, I decided. They don't know when it's dark. They don't know when they're wet. They don't know enough to quit.

Excitement stirred deep within me. With a sense of destiny, I marched toward the small brick clubhouse that guarded the entrance to the golf course.

I want to be crazy too.

I stood on the threshold of the strange room, scanning the rows of golf carts, golf clubs, and golf bags lined up along the wall. There was a glass case filled with balls and gloves, and behind it, a young man sat on a stool. He had red hair and freckles. I'd never seen so many freckles. Muscular arms bulged beneath a T-shirt.

"I'm Danny," the boy said. "Can I help you?"

"I—well—I mean—" I stepped forward. Stopped. What was I doing here anyway? "I'd like to speak to the person in charge."

"That would be my uncle, Alex McDougal. He isn't here right now, but if it's something about golf—" The voice encouraged me.

"Yes, golf. Tonight I had this urge—" I hurried, trying to cover up my nervousness. "My parents don't play, you see. And, well, I just don't know where to begin."

"How old are you?"

"Fifteen. At least almost fifteen. My birthday's at the end of June."

He nodded. "You're just under the wire. So long as you're still fourteen, you can join our Junior Golf School."

"You've got to understand. The closest I've been to golf is TV. I don't have any clubs or anything."

Danny dismissed that with a wave of his hand. "We supply the clubs and give you a playing permit. The first lesson starts tomorrow."

"So soon?"

"We get going right after school is out for the summer. There are five clinics, then a series of tournaments. Here's your entry card. Have one of your parents sign it. See you at seven."

"At least it stays light late."

"Get this," he said. "Seven in the morning."

"Ouch! This is vacation."

"Give it a try." He grinned. His teeth were strong and white against the freckled skin.

"I'll think about it." I took the card from his outstretched hand. But I had already made up

19

my mind. There was something irresistible about Danny's friendly, open face.

The alarm shrieked. I fought my way out of my dream and pressed the "off" button. I don't know which I hate worse—chalk scratching a blackboard or the shrill of an early morning alarm.

Six o'clock. Me—rise and shine and play golf at such an uncivilized hour? No way. I sank back on my pillow and pulled the sheet up to my chin and tried to recapture my dream. Instead my mind played back the real scene.

"The greatest night of my life!" Mimi had exulted as she burst into the house at midnight.

"Sh!" said Mom. "You'll wake Kate."

(As if I'd ever been asleep.)

Mimi's voice pitched higher. "Guess what? Ron and I won the dance contest!"

Even thinking about it brought on a creepy-crawly feeling.

"Only a dumb dance," I said half aloud. "Only my silly sister. Only that jerky Ron."

But it was no good. I couldn't shake that feeling. And I wasn't about to stay around and dwell on Mimi's Big Night. I planted my feet firmly on the floor, already awash with golden light. The day promised to be a scorcher, but as

I pulled on shirt and shorts, I shivered. I peeked in the fish bowl. Samson and Delilah were still inert on their bed of pebbles. I tossed them a bit of fish flake and, with a flick of their shining tails, they surfaced instantly.

"In case I never come back," I said, "I only hope Mimi remembers to feed you."

Mimi's door was ajar and I glimpsed the long dress flung over the chair and gagged on the drenching scent of perfume. I did the stairs on tiptoe, even though I knew it would take a sonic boom to rouse Mimi, and crept into the kitchen. I opened the fridge and pulled out a carton of eggs. Back went the carton. Maybe a Pop-Tart would quiet my rumbling stomach.

I eased my bike out of the garage and started pedaling. Everything looked haunted at this hour. Drawn drapes and drawn blinds gave the houses unfriendly faces, and the lawns were silvered with dew, pale as winter grass. Only the birds chirruping and plucking out worms seemed to think this was the right time to be up and doing.

I got to the park—and was I ever surprised. It wasn't only the birds. Hundreds of kids were converging on the clubhouse. And I'd thought I was doing something special signing up for a golf clinic! I joined the long line pushing toward the entrance. No such thing as a typical golfer. More boys than girls, but still lots of girls. They were short and tall (yes, some towering over me), dark and fair skinned, thin and fat, glamorous and ugly.

A heavyset girl with oily black hair elbowed her way into line ahead of me.

"Hey there!" I said, gesturing. "The end of the line for you."

"I'm just getting back my place," the girl said.

I didn't believe her, but I was new and she seemed sure so I let it pass.

"I'm Kate Morrison," I said.

"The name's Charlotte Jones, but they call me Sharkey."

It figured. The sharp teeth and the beady eyes made the nickname stick. She looked like a people eater, and I didn't want to be the one eaten up.

The line moved through the clubhouse and out the other side, inching its way toward the gate that led into the golf grounds. Danny, the redheaded boy behind the counter last night, stood at the gate checking permits.

"I'm giving it a go," I said.

"Good." A smile of recognition and he looked at my permit again as if trying to memorize my name. "Get your club over there, Kate." He pointed.

"Is that your Uncle Alex?"

Danny laughed. "Not by a long shot. That's Bix. He's a touring pro, but he's got a bum knee and he's helping us out for now."

I went over to the fence where Bix was standing. He was a commanding presence, granite jawed and steel eyed. He reminded me of someone I had seen before. He gave me a quick once-over from the top of my head to the bottom of my big feet.

"With your height and long arms," he said, passing me a club, "you can handle a long shaft and a heavy club."

I cringed. Did he have to call attention to my long arms? How I hated them. I had a mind to tell him to keep his old club and I'd head back where I came from. But home meant Mimi, and I couldn't hack that. I put the club in my hot hand and made my way over to the practice range, where I collided with a girl who was just starting her backswing.

"Sorry," I said, and jumped aside.

"I'm the one who should be sorry. I'll move over so there's room for you."

The girl had a pleasant voice and a plain face. Her fair hair was pulled back over her ears and caught in a large barrette at the nape of her neck. She was wearing a white T-shirt with the name Lora stenciled across the back. I watched her swing, fluid, graceful as a dancer.

"You've done this before," I said.

Lora nodded. "I started when I was nine, the first year they'd let me in the program, and I've come back every year for the clinics. They shape up my game for the new season."

"I'm almost fifteen and I've never held a club in my hand, well, until right now."

"It's lucky to start young—most of the pros were banging around balls as little tykes. But fifteen—that's hardly what you call ancient." Lora looked at me curiously. "When's your birthday, anyway?"

"Last day in June."

"How about that? We're almost twins. I'll be fifteen on the twenty-eighth. June is birthday month at our house. All eight of us. Ma bakes an eight-layer cake and smothers it with candles and we all celebrate together in the middle of the month." Proudly she showed me her new birthday clubs. "Did you ever see anything so beautiful? If I'm ever going to hit a big ball, it'll be this summer."

"I know what I'm getting for my birthday," I said, "and it sure isn't golf clubs." Mom had bought me a dress, but as usual the sleeves were too short and had to be let down.

"Oh, you've got to understand my father," Lora said breezily. "Some people think he's a nut, but that isn't going to change him. We could all go barefoot and hungry, but he insists we play golf in the summer and bowl in the winter. He's head coach at the university and he operates on the theory that no one ever gets into trouble if he takes his aggressions out on a ball. I just love golf, but even if I didn't, Father would make me play."

3

I laughed, and told Lora that my parents had thought I was crazy when I brought the permit home for them to sign. I imitated Mother's shocked voice. "But, Kate, whatever makes you think you want to play golf?"

Lora lifted a brow. "You mean you decided all on your own?"

"It was an impulse," I said.

"That's weird. Most parents push their kids into the golf scene. Fame and fortune on the circuit, you know, and all those golf scholarships ready and waiting—"

"Attention!" a man bellowed through a bullhorn. With his red hair and weatherbeaten face he had to be Danny's Uncle Alex. I wondered if Danny would grow up to look like him. Now *why* would I wonder about that? "Introducing Battling Bix, golf's wonder boy," the man said. "Bix had the misfortune to get in a car crash, but his bad luck is our good luck and he's here to show you the way. Now, Bix, if you'll tell us why golf is your game."

Bix stepped forward and I noticed the limp— the hesitation and the drag of his foot. But from the lines in that resolute face, I knew that it wouldn't keep him down for long.

"There's no game quite so challenging as golf," Bix said. "Win or lose, you only have yourself to blame. I got hooked when I was just about your age. Now I'd rather play than eat or sleep. I feel as if I'm wasting my life if I'm not improving my game."

"He's sure hyped up over a little old game," I said.

Lora shook her head and her ponytail bounced. "How else would he have ever made the big time?"

The bullhorn blared. "Spread out, everyone. Bix will demonstrate his winning swing. Do as he does. On the count of one, swing up. Hold it. On the count of two, swing down. The rhythm goes like this—one-is-up-and-pause-and-down."

Bix made the swing seem effortless. His shoulders turned and his hips rotated smoothly. But when I tried, my head and shoulders and hips and arms all seemed to be operating on a different set of hinges.

Alex circulated up and down the rows. He stopped and helped me. "Move your left hand on top of the club," he said, "so you can see the first three knuckles. It's a little thing, but golf is a game of tiny adjustments."

I waited until Alex was out of earshot and then I turned to Lora. "Gosh, is this ever uncomfortable!"

"Oh, you'll get used to it." Lora nodded. "Actually my golf grip feels so right I'm having trouble holding a baseball bat." Lora giggled. "Yes, we all play baseball too. You should see my mother sliding into home plate."

The thought of Mom sliding anyplace cracked me up. "That'll be the day," I said.

The clinic was over. The time had gone fast. I went over to the fence to turn in my club.

"First time out?" Bix asked.

I gulped. So my clumsiness had been a stand-out all the way across the range! With those hundreds of kids, I had been the biggest klutz.

"I'm hopeless." I handed back my club.

"Keep it," Bix said. "Go home and practice. Stand with your feet a little farther apart— about the width of your shoulders. That will give you better balance. And keep your left arm straight on the backswing. Think of a pendulum swinging back and forth and keep that rhythm."

"Yes, sir." If I'd been wearing boots, I would have clicked my heels.

He dismissed me. "If you care enough to give the game your best effort, I predict you will become a very fine golfer. You have a long arc."

I walked away in a daze. I looked around for Lora and found her at the bike rack.

"Say, Lora, what's a long arc?"

"Move your hands down the shaft of the club, and you'll swing the club in a shorter arc than you would if you hold on to the grip where your hands belong." Lora demonstrated. "See. Your club is longer than mine. Your arms are longer too, so naturally you can swing the club in a bigger arc, and every inch of arc adds that much more power and distance."

I dropped my arms to my side—the long arms

I despised. Now I'd been told they were an asset.

After sweating out the golf clinic and the bike ride home, it was a treat to step into the cool dimness of our front hall. Mom was waiting for me.

"How did it go?" she asked. She looked fresh and pretty in her white blouse and print skirt nipped in at her tiny waist. Just seeing her made me feel really tacky.

"A big scene," I said, and shoved the club Bix had given me into the closet. "Zillions of kids."

"Oh?" Mom's neat little brows shot up in surprise. "Did you learn anything?"

"I learned there's lots about the game I don't know."

"That's to be expected. But it was fun, I hope."

"Like they say, there's good news, and there's bad news. The bad news. Most of the kids in the program have been there before and they have a jump on me. The good news. Tall girls with long arms aren't considered freaks in the golf arena."

"Kate, what a terrible thing to say!"

"Well, maybe no one comes right out with it. But it's a feeling I get around here."

"Darling, I can't imagine why. We all want the best for you."

"Sure," I said. How could the Beautiful People know what it feels like to be a clod?

"I'm on my way to the store," Mom said. "If Mimi wakes up, tell her I'll be back in an hour or so." A comforting pat on my arm. "It must have been exhausting in all this heat. Rest a bit, hon. There's a slice of watermelon in the fridge just for you."

The watermelon was pink, ripe, and deliciously cold. With the first bite I began to revive.

A patter of feet on the floor above. Like a pale ghost, Mimi drifted into the dining room, silken hair cascading around her shoulders, eyes half closed. With a world-weary sigh, she dropped down into the chair opposite me.

"That kind of party drains you, really drains you," she said.

I concentrated on plucking the shiny black seeds out of the melon and stacking them on the edge of the plate.

"Ron's a tiger. Now that I think of it, it's not surprising we won the dance contest."

"I don't want to hear about it all over again."

"Again?"

"You gave a blow-by-blow account in the middle of the night and I'm not deaf."

But Mimi wouldn't be turned off. "He does this thing in double time, then a hesitation and back on beat. I said, 'Ron, you're born with a beat,' and he said to me, 'Yeah, I know.'"

I choked down a cube of melon. "Cute," I said.

The phone rang. Mimi sprang up and flew down the hall into the TV room.

"Ron," she shrilled in an adoring voice, "you told me you'd wait until noon to call. For all you know you might have awakened me, and I'm not my best self when someone wakes me up."

I stifled the scream that was forming in my throat. I marched into the hall and removed the golf club from the closet. I marched back through the dining room and out the patio doors into the garden. The garden was a pretty place, with a well-tended grass plot surrounded by a rose garden, carefully nurtured by Mother with plant foods and insecticides, each bush tagged with a lovely name—White Bouquet, Tropicana, Eclipse, and my favorite, Peace, yellow petals dipped in pink.

Usually I found the garden a pleasant retreat,

a place to relax and meditate. Not so today. Pressure was building up in my chest, rattling my rib cage. With a mighty swing I cranked up the club and smashed it down. Pow! The jolt sent a shooting pain up my arm.

"Ow-ow-ow-owie!" My voice bleeped like an ambulance in the night.

"What is it, Kate?"

I spun around, surprised to see Mr. Dubois, gardening in the heat.

"A mishap," I said, walking over to the fence. "I'm supposed to swing like a pendulum, but I got sort of mixed up—(mad was more like it)—and I swung like a woodchopper with an ax."

"Better do your swinging over here," Mr. Dubois said. "Your father won't take kindly to your putting craters in his lawn, but I'd consider it a favor if you dug up the moss and crabgrass on our side." When I hesitated, he said, "Besides, there's lots of shade and it's no day to be exercising in the sun."

"I'll buy that."

"Take the gate," Mr. Dubois said.

"No, I'm coming over just the way I used to."

I climbed the fence, thinking back on all the times I'd gone back and forth—not lately, of course, but as a little girl. Mr. Dubois had rigged up a swing on the limb of the giant oak and had sunk an old tub in the ground and called it a wading pool. He taught me to tell time by reading the changing shadows on the sundial and how to read the words across the face: COUNT NONE BUT SUNNY HOURS. He showed me how to shell peas and husk corn, and he gave me a kitten, and then, when the kitten scratched Mimi and Mom said it had to go, he took it back so I could play with it.

"Good to be back," I said as I hopped to the ground.

"When you've no young'uns of your own, it's nice to borrow someone else's," he said.

I moved into the shade of the old oak, and Mr. Dubois followed me.

"How long have you been playing golf?" he asked.

"All of an hour," I said, and laughed at his startled expression. In a burst of confidence I told him about Lora's flowing swing and my awkward one and how Bix had tried to encourage me. "Can you believe it? He wants me to swing the club a thousand times before the next clinic. Just swing to get the rhythm. No ball, or I can use one of those puffballs that go no place. I'll try that tomorrow."

"Too much in this heat." Mr. Dubois shook his head.

"I've got to catch up with the others."

"Well, when you've had enough, come into the house for some lemonade with Angel and me." Mrs. Dubois's name was Evangelina, but Mr. Dubois called her Angel, even though her long straight nose and straight cropped hair hardly suited.

"I just might do that," I said.

I took a deep breath. It was like sucking in the air from a blast furnace. No matter. I felt relaxed now, the tension gone. "One and two," I counted, but at the first waggle of the club, a squirrel scolded—*chatter, chatter*—which I took to mean, "Get lost, lady. This is my tree."

"You'll just have to put up with me." I arched my back. "I'm learning golf, you know."

I had no idea how long I'd been practicing when a sudden movement by the fence caught my eye. I stopped swinging and turned. Ron!

"I could do without an audience," I snapped.

"Hasn't anyone told you it's a hundred in the shade?"

"I'm fully aware of the heat."

"Well, you shouldn't be swinging a club. You'll get sunstroke." The golden voice made even the most banal suggestion sound like a poetry reading. But I was in no mood for poetry.

"So now you're concerned over my welfare."

"Of course I am." The engaging smile. "Mimi and I are on our way to the beach."

Humph, I thought nastily. I hope you both drown.

Ron leaned on the fence looking at me with those beautiful dark eyes, his hands out-stretched—expressive hands that made every little gesture meaningful.

"Now, Kate, before the heat gets you, come along with us for a swim."

My heart lifted. Ron had asked me to go with him. I felt the cool water caressing my hot skin. I saw the beach towel spread out across the sand, the two of us, side by side, on our own terry-cloth island, alone.

Mimi's sweet voice chimed from the patio, "Ron. Oh, Ron—what's keeping you?"

"Run along," I said. "I have other plans." With the back of my hand I wiped the perspiration from my forehead, and when Ron was out of sight I went on swinging.

No beach towel was big enough for the three of us.

4

B<small>ACK</small> again," I said, smiling at Danny. I was so close to him that I could have counted every freckle on his face. Now I've never been too keen on freckles, but on him they looked good—even handsome in a natural sort of way.

"I knew it." Danny grinned and stamped S<small>ECOND</small> C<small>LINIC</small> on my permit card. He returned it to me. "Bix wants to see you," he said.

"Me?"

"Yeah." Danny cocked his head and I noticed that even his ears had freckles. "He's over there. At the range."

Bix saw me before I saw him.

"Have you been practicing?" he asked.

"A few zillion times."

"Show me."

I glanced over my shoulder. "Too many people around."

That must have been the wrong thing to say. Bix lit into me.

"If you play golf, there'll always be people around—partners, opponents, caddies. And if you're ever lucky enough to compete in a tournament, the starter will announce your name and you'll tee off with the entire field looking on."

"I could never do that."

"How long would anyone last on tour if he let every little thing distract him? Crowds cannot always be controlled. It's a matter of concentration, Kate. Block everything out but golf." He flicked away a bee zigzagging between us, but I knew if his ball were in play, he wouldn't let a mere bee divert him. "Now let's see that swing," he said.

The swing jerked.

"Again."

I brought the club back for a second try, and all the practicing I'd done in the heat of the day, and even after dark, made my muscles respond rhythmically.

Bix nodded. "Better. I can only help those

who help themselves, and you're making an effort." Abruptly he turned and limped off.

Lora rushed to my side. "Lucky you." Her eyes were bright and her cheeks flushed. "No secrets. What's it all about?"

"Bix wanted to see me swing, that's all."

"There must be more to it than that."

"I think he's testing me. He told me to practice and he wanted to be sure I had."

"I wish he'd test me too." Lora sounded wistful.

"He doesn't need to. Your swing is perfect the way it is.

"I don't get enough distance. That's what kept me from making the Junior District last year."

"What's so big about the District?"

"Like everything. I've played this course so many times I know every bush and every tree. But if I were in the District, I'd play a different course each week with the top Junior players from all around." Her voice rose enthusiastically as she described the woods, the streams, the ravines of a course she'd once played in Shenfield Hills. "What a challenge! What a treat!"

I liked Lora. I only wished there was some way I could go along with her to the exciting places she was talking about—but what chance has a beginner? I thought of Aunt Lucy and Uncle Robb. They lived in Shenfield Hills. I sighed. Wouldn't you know—they didn't play golf.

"Hurry, Kate." Lora skipped ahead. "The clinic's starting."

I began to jog, but a hefty shoulder jostled me off the path. "Teacher's pet!"

The words stung. I turned to Lora. "Do you know that girl?"

"Sharkey? Who doesn't? We've been in the same clinics and on the same golf course playing together for six years." Lora frowned. "But I can't figure her out. I've asked her over to my house, but she won't come, and no one's ever been asked to her place. I hear her father beat it, but no one's seen her mother either. It's one big mystery. She's got to be hiding something."

"But why should she be mad at me when I don't even know her?"

"The fact that Bix singled you out is reason enough to rattle her." Lora eyed me. "She's a tough one to play with. She wants to win so much, she hassles you the whole way."

"What do you mean by that?"

"You'll find out soon enough."

Bix held aloft a club with a metal head. "Woods are for distance," he said. "Irons are for accuracy." He spread out a set of irons on the ground. "There are ten irons. The lower the number of the iron, the farther the ball will go. The higher the number of the iron, the more the face is laid back, and that angled face makes the ball go higher, over trees and traps, so naturally these irons are used for short shots, especially approaching the green."

Bix picked up a club and passed it around the circle. "Here's a five iron, the workhorse in your bag. You will use it for that medium shot, for getting out of the rough, for a bad lie on the fairway."

"It's my favorite." Lora stroked the club head fondly. "That's because I hit it on the sweet spot."

Sweet spot. I liked the sound. Evidently some clubs were easier to hit with than others. I wondered what my favorite club would be.

Bix gestured. "If you need an iron for the clinic, Danny's passing them out."

Danny chose an iron for me.

"Another trial run," I said.

"Don't give me that. I saw Bix corner you. He doesn't waste his time on just anyone."

So Danny had noticed too! For Lora,

41

Sharkey, and now Danny, attention from Bix had special significance. I felt excited. I strained to hear every word Bix was saying. Swinging an iron wasn't all that different from swinging a wood. The club was shorter, yes, and that made me stand up straighter. But the grip was the same, and the ball was positioned the same too—off the left heel with the right foot moved in closer.

Bix tossed Danny a ball. "Now watch Danny," he said, and when Danny drilled the ball out beyond the last range marker, even Bix seemed impressed.

"Wow!" I nudged Lora. "Did you see that?"

"Didn't you know? Danny won the Juniors last year."

"Now, Lora," Bix said, "show us what you can do."

Lora stepped up in front of the group and sent the ball flying down the middle of the range.

"I'm proud of both of you," Bix said. "You are proof that a public park can turn out championship golfers. Now for someone new." He looked at me and beckoned.

"I've never hit a golf ball. Only those little puff things. I wouldn't have the faintest—"

A determined finger pointed. "There's always a first time."

I stumbled forward. Concentrate, Bix had said. Block everything out.

Bix placed a ball in front of me. It looked awfully small. My mind whirred with disjointed thoughts—the grip, the stance, the more upright swing for an iron. The palms of my hands dripped. But I knew I had to go through with it. I brought the club back. One-is-up-and-pause-and— *Wham!* I did it! I hit the ball!

A roar. Screams. Startled, I looked up. The ball was careening off sideways, almost at right angles to where I stood, barely missing the crowd along the sidelines. It struck someone. Danny! His hand flew to his forehead. Blood!

I gasped. My very first golf shot had hit Danny. He was injured. My heart plummeted.

"Now you'll get it!" Sharkey shrieked.

I stood paralyzed.

Bix moved toward Danny. "Are you hurt?"

"Heck, no! It's only my head."

Bix spoke tersely. "You know better than to stand in front of a person who is hitting a ball. It's not only bad manners, it can be dangerous."

"I'm not about to do it again." Danny swabbed his head with a handkerchief.

Bix waved for quiet. "You have just seen a shank, a freak shot. The ball just happens to hit the hosel instead of the face of the club. On occasion, even the pros shank—the most demoralizing shot in golf. There are several possible causes for a shank." I wasn't listening. I cut through the crowd to Danny. The bleeding had stopped, but already there was a nasty lump near the temple.

"Sorry, sorry," I said. "Is there anything I can do? Believe me, I didn't mean—"

"Sure about that?" He laughed easily as if the whole thing were a huge joke.

I focused on the purple-red lump. I felt ill.

"I never do anything right," I said. "No matter what I try, it turns out wrong. I should never have tried to play golf in the first place. And for sure I should never have hit a ball with so many people around. Something disastrous was bound to happen."

"Nothing disastrous. Now if you can just harness all that power and hit the ball straight instead of angling it—"

"I'm not hitting a ball ever again," I said. I ran out the gate. I hopped on my bike and pedaled hard. I didn't even slow down when I heard Danny calling my name. I didn't have Mimi to blame for this. I had done it myself.

The old klutz. And to about the nicest boy I had ever met.

The note propped against the sugar bowl read: KATE! ALERT! IMPORTANT MESSAGE. MIMI.

I tripped over a cord and knew that she couldn't be far away. Mimi could always be found at the end of a cord—a telephone cord, a hair dryer cord, an extension cord. The cord at my feet snaked across the dining room rug, under the patio doors, and out to a portable hi-fi in the sunny center of the garden. Mimi was lying face down beside the hi-fi in a floppy hat and a bikini.

"What gives?" I shouted.

Mimi cut the decibels.

"A *boy*"—Mimi's voice underlined boy— "wanted you to phone the minute you got home."

"That hardly calls for a conference. The name and number will do."

"The name's Danny and here's the phone number."

I froze. Why was Danny calling me? Did he have a concussion after all? And it was all my doing.

I spun around, but Mimi reached out and stopped me.

"I didn't know you were dating anyone," she said.

"Who said anything about dating? Danny's helping out at the golf course and I shanked a ball and hit him in the head."

Mimi sat bolt upright. "Now that's a new way to meet someone. I would never have thought of that."

"For Pete's sake," I said. "I didn't think of it. It was all a gruesome mistake."

"Did he think you did it on purpose? Was he really hurt or just a little mad?"

"I'm about to find out."

Mimi arched a brow and asked with interest, "Is he cute?"

Was Danny cute? I guess he was. He certainly had about the nicest smile I had ever seen on any boy. I liked his voice too—warm and kind of enthusiastic. However, I certainly wasn't about to share this information with glamour puss. Aloud I said, "He's good at golf. That's his claim to fame."

"I don't know any golfers," Mimi said, as if part of her education were slighted, "but I wouldn't mind meeting one."

Inside the TV room I waited, only a matter of seconds, until Mimi switched up the volume on the hi-fi. I dialed Danny's number, and as soon as I heard his voice I asked anxiously, "How's the head?"

"My head's fine, but your swing's hurting. Now if you'll come over to the football field, we'll get you straightened out."

"Football field?"

"At North High. Now that school's out, it's a great place to practice and much closer to you than the park."

"I just gave up the game," I said.

"That's what I like, a quitter."

"It's smart to quit before the damage suits start."

"Come off it," Danny said. "You heard Bix. He said it was all my fault, and he blitzed me again after you left." Danny lowered his voice, and I caught the rasp of irritation. "Will you, or won't you, meet us at North in twenty minutes?"

It was the first time I had heard Danny use that tone and I found I didn't like it.

"Us?" I played for time.

"Lora's with me."

"I'll think about it," I said.

"If you're not there, we'll come and get you."

"Don't do that!" I said promptly. If they came anywhere near the house, Bikini Mimi was sure to get into the act. And this was one guy I was determined not to share. "I'm on my way."

I pedaled in high gear, but Danny and Lora were at the football field ahead of me.

"Whatcha do, fly?"

"Bix brought us," Lora said, "and Bix drives at one speed—wide open."

I checked Danny's forehead. "It looks somewhat better."

"Packed it in ice and, *zap,* the bump's gone."

"Not quite."

"Forget it," Danny said, and flipped open a canvas bag. Hundreds of golf balls cascaded onto the grass.

"What did you do," I said, "rob the shop?"

Lora looked at Danny proudly. "Old Hawkeye finds balls where no one else ever sees them. Even spotted a ball in the crotch of a tree and shinnied up after it."

"Yeah, and it was hardly worth the trip." He picked a couple of balls at random. "See, this one has a crack in the casing, and this one looks more like an egg than a ball. No one could putt with that. But it's okay for banging around." He teed the ball up in front of me and handed me a driver. "Go ahead. Hit it. Won't matter at all if you lose it."

I stood over the ball, staring at it. Finally I

backed off. "Thanks just the same. But I'm psyched. I know I'm going to shank again, and I want none of that."

Danny pulled a quarter out of his pocket. He flipped it and the silver glinted in the sun. "Bet you a quarter that you can't shank, no matter what."

"Of course I can!" I tossed my head and my hair flew out from under the headband.

"Don't bet," Lora cried. "It's a trick."

"If I could shank once," I said, "I can do it again. Obviously I've got a shank swing." I raised my hand. "Stand back everyone." I pivoted my hips, turned my shoulders and, coiling up like a spring, powered the club head through the ball. A sharp smack, a sizzle of wind. For a moment I didn't see anything, then my eyes followed the ball's soaring flight over the far goal post, the high bounce, the hop forward, and it was gone from sight.

"Wow!" Danny whistled.

"Wow!" Lora said.

"Wow!" I said immodestly. I knew I'd never be the same again.

I tried another ball, swinging with abandon. How could I explain this thing happening inside me? My body, taut, unforgiving like a door jammed shut, was suddenly free.

Lora and Danny began hitting balls too, and soon the green field was polka-dotted with white.

A horn sounded. Bix.

"So soon," I said with regret.

"It's been over an hour," Danny said. "It just doesn't seem that long."

We ran around the field gathering up balls until the canvas bag was full.

"You win," I told Danny. "I don't have a quarter with me, but I'll pay off at the next clinic."

"I warned you," Lora said knowingly.

"The bet was a gimmick," Danny said. "Just something to get you going. Shanks are crazy shots. You might not shank again for the rest of your life."

"No matter. I'll pay up. Believe me, it was a pleasure not to shank."

"I can't take your money," Danny said. "It was a con game. Lora knew it. It's impossible to shank with a wood. You can only shank an iron."

I laughed. "So that's it! But you'll get your reward for outsmarting me." I tried to sound menacing, but the attempt was unconvincing. I felt too happy.

5

The football field became my home away from home. Mom and Mimi couldn't understand what was so great about hitting balls down a field. But when things got sticky around our place, I found release in the big freewheeling swing. I liked that go-for-broke feeling the power hit gave me. I also liked the feeling of Danny's support and encouragement.

The short shots didn't do that for me, and I didn't pay all that much attention at the third clinic. Bix must have noticed my halfhearted efforts at chipping and pitching and he pounced on me before I got through the gate. With Lora by my side and Sharkey across the path giving me the Evil Eye, I felt like a worm with no hole to crawl into.

"It's more fun to hit hard," I said defensively.

"For the time being"—Bix's eyes snapped—"deny yourself that pleasure. It's the days that your chips roll up to the pin and the days that your putts drop that you score well. Your short game is the payoff. Practice it."

"I'll do that," I said meekly.

"I have the perfect place to practice," Lora said. "Come over to my house and I'll show you."

"Sure," I said. We walked through the clubhouse. "Where's Danny? I want to pay him the quarter I owe him."

"Danny's taking the day off," Lora said, and I wondered how she knew as I struggled to suppress a stab of jealousy.

We took off on our bikes for the old section of town. At one time the houses had been grand, but now they were falling apart, with sagging windows and sagging porches, peeling paint, and rusty fences. A skinny dog fastened to a long chain barked as we went by.

"Poor dog," I said, and sighed. "Poor me."

"Hey, what's bugging you?"

"Bix didn't exactly cheer me up. I've been

working hard. I just get the long shot going, and now he tells me that it's the little game that counts."

"Bix is telling it like it is. You're lucky to have all that power. It gets you nearer the green so you can use a shorter iron. But you still have to finish the hole. The pro who hits farther than anyone else has never won a single tournament."

"How come?"

"Just as I was saying. He gets right up to the green, then he blows it. There's an old saying— 'Drive for show, putt for dough.'"

"Okay, okay," I said.

Lora spun the wheels of her bike to a stop on a gravel drive. "Welcome," she said.

If anything, her house was older and uglier than the others on the block, but the front lawn was wide and green with a neatly clipped hedge. A tall boy in a flowered shirt and sandals was pushing a mower.

"Say, Brian," Lora called. "Where's Ma?"

"How should I know?"

"The car's gone. Didn't she say where she was going?"

"I forget."

Lora groaned. "That big brother of mine was born impossible and time hasn't done a thing

53

for him." She held a side door open. I found myself in a hall lined with lockers, each labeled by name. I wondered how my parents would cope with a family of eight, then gave up. Plenty of problems with just the two of us.

"Daddy built these," Lora said with a flourish as she set her golf bag inside a cubicle marked LORA. "In fact, he built almost everything around here." She led the way into the living room. "See? He designed all the furniture. Early American Survival, he calls it, and so far even Brian and his kooky pals haven't smashed it up."

I tried out a sturdy straight-back chair with a hammock seat.

"Daddy operates on the theory that if there's no overstuffed furniture we're more apt to get our homework done."

"It's what you're conditioned to," I said. "Mimi says she can only study lying down."

"I take it Mimi's your sister."

I nodded. "But you'd never know we're related. She's cute and pretty."

"We've got one of those too. Number three girl." The way she said it, I could tell she wasn't in the least concerned that her sister was pretty and she was plain. I clasped and unclasped my hands. Why couldn't I feel that way?

54

"Now for the obstacle course."

At first glance the backyard seemed bleak—a small field without a tree or a flower—but then I made out all kinds of interesting items—hoops, stakes, a sand pit, and in the corner a patch of smooth bent grass, a putting green.

"Here's where we start." Lora placed a ball in back of a white tape. "The object is to pitch the ball into the bushel basket." With a click of the club, Lora lofted the ball into the basket.

"Try it," Lora said.

"I don't have a wedge."

"Here. Use mine. But when the tournaments start, you'll want your own clubs. Those free ones are okay, but you'll do better with a matched set. They don't need to be new—just the right length and the right weight."

"I'm broke," I said.

"Tough." Lora showed no sympathy. "For my first set of clubs I sold Christmas cards, wheeled an old lady, baby-sat—"

I made a face. "Oh, I couldn't do that. There are two monsters down the block—"

"Why not?" Lora said. "With your big swing, I'd make the effort."

I moved over to the tape and tried to gauge the distance to the bushel basket. Lora had made it look so easy. But it wasn't easy for me.

My first shot zoomed into the middle of the yard.

"The touch of an elephant," I said, moaning.

On the fifth try the ball dropped into the basket.

"See?" Lora said. "It's just as Bix told you. Short shots are a matter of practice." Lora crossed over to a sand trap. "But give me a trap shot, and I'm psyched." Lora stepped down into the sand, wiggling her feet around for a firmer stance. "The trick is in pretending the ball is a fried egg and lifting it out whole."

I giggled.

Lora cocked her wrists and slammed into the sand too far back of the ball, and the ball spun up, then fell back into the trap.

"See what I mean?" Lora climbed out of the trap. "I know what to do, but show me sand and I goof. Enough is enough. C'mon, Kate, before I perish of thirst."

I eyed the trap. I would have liked to have tried a sand shot, but Lora was already heading toward the house, and reluctantly I followed her into the kitchen.

"What will it be?" Lora swung the door of the giant refrigerator wide. The top shelf was crammed with every kind of juice imaginable.

"I'm ape for grape," I said.

A voice boomed through the screen door. "Same for me." Brian stuck his head inside. A mass of black ringlets, and wouldn't you know, Lora's hair straight as string.

"Help yourself, Mr. Helpless," Lora said.

"Geez, I do all the work around here, and that's the thanks I get."

Lora scoffed. "The only time you do anything is when someone puts a pistol to your head." But she poured the juice into a paper cup and handed it to him.

"And Danny'll want his usual," Brian called from outside the door.

"Danny?" Twin spots of color crimsoned Lora's cheeks.

"Yup. He's coming up the driveway now."

Lora rushed to the door. "So he is."

"Hang around, Danny boy," Brian said. "I'll be done with this lousy lawn in just a minute and then we can escape." The mower started up with a noisy sputter, the sound receding as Brian moved away.

Lora held open the screen and smiled. "Come in, Danny. Have a little something with us while you wait."

"Us?"

"Kate's here. We've been messing around the obstacle course."

Danny stepped into the kitchen, and I thought how much bigger he looked indoors—like a Christmas tree that's been brought inside and takes over a whole room.

"Hi, Kate," he said.

"I was looking for you." I dug into my pocket. The quarter was still there, warm from the heat of my body. "Catch!" I said and flipped the coin.

"I told you the bet was off."

"I insist."

"Okay, and I insist on taking you out on the town and blowing all of it on you."

"Big deal."

Lora handed Danny a tall glass of lemonade with a fresh slice of lemon floating on top. "The usual," she said.

"Thanks, Lora. Hits the spot." Glass in hand, Danny went out the door. "See if I can get the guy moving."

"Isn't that asking a bit much?" Lora said, but already Danny was out of earshot.

"I take it Danny and Brian are buddies." The question was tactful but loaded. I congratulated myself on my Mata Hari tactics.

"Forever almost." Lora sat down on the kitchen stool. "They joined the Indian Guides at the age of four and as the motto goes, 'pals forever,' although I can't see why. Brian is so lazy he won't reach for a Kleenex and he thinks he's an irresistible Don Juan. One girl after another. With Danny it's golf, not girls. But I just happen to know several girls who think he's terrific and he doesn't even register."

It didn't take much imagination on my part to know that Lora was one of the girls who wanted to be on Danny's list.

The door rattled and Lora's hands flew to her throat.

"Okay if I leave my glass right here?" Danny set it down on the counter. "We're on our way. So long, Kate."

"Aren't you going to say goodbye to me?" Lora asked.

"Sure, but we'll be back in a couple of hours so it'll be hello and goodbye all over again."

Footsteps receded down the drive. Lora sighed. "Danny thinks I go with the house, a fixture not worth noticing." Suddenly she threw back her head and laughed. "I've never thought of it before. Danny's just like the mule in that joke."

"Never heard a mule joke."

"Ah, but you're about to. Farmer Jones sold a mule to his friend, but the friend couldn't make the mule budge so he complained.

'There's nothing the matter with that mule,' Farmer Jones said, and he hit the mule over the head with a board. The mule began to move. 'But why did you hit him over the head?' the friend asked. 'He's a perfectly good mule,' Farmer Jones assured his friend. 'You just got to get his attention.'"

Lora stood up and clinked my glass. "Here's to you and Danny. You hit him on the head. You got his attention."

"You don't understand. Danny's nothing to me, and hitting him on the head was the last thing—"

"Nevertheless, it was a lucky shot," Lora said.

I certainly agreed with her about that. And I was glad that Lora had been frank about her relationship with Danny. It meant a lot to me to have as good a friend as Lora. I could just imagine Mimi the Moocher saying something like that. *Fat chance.* I would have to make sure she never got her beautifully manicured paws on Danny. It had been bad enough with Ron.

After I left Lora my mind was like a popcorn machine, popping off in every direction. I liked Danny. Lora liked Danny. Yet Lora, Danny, and I were still friends. I liked Ron. Ron liked Mimi. But Ron had cut me off, a nice clean break. How did I really feel about him now? Did I want to be his friend?

"Don't think about it," I told myself.

Golf, my refuge, my escape.

I swung into the Dubois drive and leaned my bike against the old oak. Through the branches I could see the clouds puffing along across the blue sky. Mr. Dubois came around the corner of the house with a Shasta daisy for me.

"How's the golf, Kate?"

He seemed really interested, so I told him about my big swing and my bad short game and the obstacle course at Lora's.

"I have just the spot where you can build a trap, back by the tool shed. Even have the sand for it."

I hesitated, wondering if I were asking too much. "Would it be all right with you if I brought the Gillespie boys over with me? I'm trying to earn money for my own set of clubs."

"Might as well ask 'em over." Mr. Dubois's old eyes twinkled. "They're running wild through here most times anyway."

I phoned and Mrs. Gillespie's voice rose in joyous crescendo. "An angel sent from heaven! I'm falling apart. I just put the milk in the broom closet and the detergent in the icebox. My dear, come the soonest."

Some kook, I thought, but aloud I said, "We'll be digging in the Dubois yard, so dress the boys in old clothes."

Ten minutes later I rang the bell and a lady in pink curlers shoved Charles and Cecil onto the porch.

"Whatever you do," Mrs. Gillespie crooned, "don't rush into marriage. Single is bliss."

"I haven't given the matter much thought," I said, but she was already closing the door in my face.

"Hang on to them as long as you can. I need sleep."

I led the way down the walk.

"I'm King Kong," Charles said, "and him is Brother Rat."

"Not neither." Rat punched Kong and Kong punched back.

"Save your strength," I said. "We have work to do. We're building a sand trap."

"Kings don't work," Kong said.

"Well, sit in your rickshaw and watch me work."

A yowl. "You said we could dig."

"You're the one who said you didn't want to work."

"Digging's not work," Kong said.

Feeling unhinged, I herded them into the

Dubois backyard. Mr. Dubois had lined up an assortment of garden tools—a small spade and a trowel for the boys and a big spade and a pitchfork for me.

The topsoil was easy excavating, but the stratum of hard-packed clay was something else. Hot, heavy work. The boys soon became bored and the slugging resumed.

"Boys! I have a super idea!" Once upon a time Mr. Dubois had introduced me to the diverting art of making mud pies. Now, with a bucket of water and mud for the asking, the boys settled down to hurling mud missiles at each other and an occasional one at me.

Mimi's voice drifted across the fence. "Now you'd better believe me—"

I straightened, my fingers tightening around the handle of the spade. Mimi dressed in white and Ron by her side, clean shaven with hip-hugging cotton cords so new they looked stiff. He stared.

"Meet the Mud Queen." I made a mock bow.

"But, Kate, why are you digging a ditch?"

"This may look like a ditch to you, but it's a sand trap."

A tinkling laugh and Mimi said, "You won't ever catch me digging—"

"And I won't catch you being a great golfer

either." I caught my breath. What had made me say that—as if I were on my way to golfing fame, when actually I'd yet to play my first round?

A shriek.

"Mimi!" Ron said. "What is it?"

"Those rotten kids!" She shrieked again. "Look at me. Mud from head to foot. And they did it de-lib-er-ate-ly." She ran toward the house, pausing on the patio. "I'm going to call Mrs. Gillespie and tell her to keep her brats at home."

"Don't bother," I said. "I'm in charge."

"Then do something!" Mimi wailed.

I waited until she was inside and then I walked toward Charles. He looked a little cowed. He'd probably been beaten plenty. But I only gave him a love pat.

"Charles," I said, "you have a fine pitching arm."

Ron chuckled, that special chuckle that always got me, but it didn't quite come off.

"Kate," he said, "how come you're on this golf kick?"

"I owe it all to you." I smiled sweetly.

He rocked back on his heels. "I don't get it. I don't even play golf."

"Nevertheless," I said, "you got me started."

6

Bix must have noticed my confusion.

"This is only a practice round, Kate, and I've told Lora to help you in any way she can. But next week when the tournaments start you'll be on your own, so listen carefully."

Lora stepped up on a mound of earth, the tee. The tee was the starting-off place, and there was a tee at the beginning of each of the eighteen holes.

"First thing to remember," Lora said, "is to stay away from that trap on the right. See, I'm lining myself up with my shoulders and feet square to the left side of the fairway." She swung, and the ball soared just where she'd aimed it, straight as an arrow, in perfect position for her next shot.

Bix nodded. "Good, Lora. You've got the kind of grooved swing that will hold up under pressure. I expect this year you'll make the District."

"Really, Bix? Oh, I hope—" Her scrubbed face lighted up in an ear-to-ear smile. I leaned over and pressed the little wooden peg—Lora called the peg a tee—into the ground and placed my ball on top of it.

"Careful, Kate," Bix said. "You may tee up as much as two club lengths back of the markers, but not so much as an inch in front of them."

My heart began to pound. One thing to swing a golf club in a clinic, to practice in the Dubois yard, or to mess around Lora's place. But now each stroke had to be marked down. If I whiffed the ball or topped it or heeled it, the stroke had to be counted. There were no "overs" in golf.

I could feel Bix's eyes on me, and now others crowded around. Sharkey pushed her way to the front.

"How come Kate gets to go off ahead of me? I've been in the clinics longer than her. How come I gotta wait around?"

My stomach churned. I glanced at Bix. He acted as if there had been no interruption at all.

"Slow down, Kate," he said. "In times of tension, a player tends to speed up the swing."

I tried again.

"That's it," he said.

Bix had a miraculous effect on me. I wanted to give him my best. This time I made myself pause at the top. I shifted my weight and smashed through the ball. I shaded my eyes with my hand and followed the flight of the ball as it headed— Oh, no! Not the trap that Lora had warned me about! Stupid me! How could I forget so soon? But before my unbelieving eyes the ball sailed right over the trap. It bounced on the back lip and hurtled forward into the rough, yards ahead of Lora's ball.

"Great shot," Bix said, "but you're pressing your luck. Lora is playing the percentages, avoiding the trap. Think about it." He handed each of us a score card. "Play well. Have fun. And when you finish, bring your cards to me in the clubhouse."

I set off along the fairway, singing a nameless tune. The ground was springy underfoot, like walking on a sponge. The trees were even more lush and full, thanks to a good wet spring and the hot summer weather which was now in full swing.

"Hey there!" Lora admonished. "You're supposed to stay back of the ball, and my ball's farthest back."

"That's one item I should remember." My hand flew to my forehead, the spot where I'd clobbered Danny with my shanked ball.

Lora said, "It's still a long way to the green. I'll take a wood for this shot." As always, she hit the ball right down the middle.

I paced off thirty yards to my ball, each stride a small triumph. Had I really outdriven Lora by that much? Suppose in my very first round of golf I racked up some sort of record. I'd dreamed of this moment. Me. Ms. Success.

My ball was sitting up on the crown of a weed. I swung hard. I did it again! Outdistanced Lora. What a great round this was going to be.

"Big. Way up by the green." There was a note of awe in Lora's voice. We walked a little closer. "Only hope you're not in trouble," she said.

"Trouble?"

"Golf courses are designed so that if you get off the fairway and into the rough, you're apt to find an obstacle in your way."

"I see what you mean." My way was blocked by the drooping branch of an elm. I frowned. "I thought they planted trees to make the golf course pretty, not to make life miserable."

"Not miserable," Lora corrected. "Interesting."

"Well, what am I supposed to do?" I stared at the offending branch.

"You have a choice," Lora said. "Punch the ball under the branch with a flat-faced iron or take a lofted iron and get the ball into the air fast and fly it over the branch."

"I'll try the up and over."

The ball lifted, heading for the flagstick—what looked to be a perfect shot. But it didn't carry quite far enough. It nose-dived into a trap by the green.

I groaned.

"Bad break," Lora said.

I climbed down into the trap, glad now that I'd been practicing in my homemade trap. I spun the ball out and it sat down in the fluff growing along the edge of the green.

"Bravo!" Lora said. "You got out on the first try."

"But I don't like this lie."

My shot didn't quite come off and it took three putts to get into the hole. How had it happened? My drive had been spectacular—way out beyond Lora's—and my second shot had been longer than hers too. But it was Lora who had carded the five and I was the one with an eight.

Hours later, I staggered off the course, my dream shattered. I had scored 156 strokes to Lora's 90.

"I'm tearing up my card." I said. "I don't want Bix to see it."

But Bix shoved a large loose-leaf notebook at me. "Mark down your score with the date," he said, "and every time you play, enter your score here. Then we can work out a handicap for you."

"I don't want a record of this round," I said.

"We have a rule. All scores must be posted. It isn't a question of what you can shoot or what you want to shoot, it's a matter of what you did shoot."

Reluctantly I scratched the three-digit score opposite my name. I'd hoped golf would be a cure-all for all my disappointments. But a big swing wasn't enough. Placing one weary foot ahead of the other, I made for the exit.

Loser again.

"Hey, Kate!" A voice from another planet. "Did you have a good game?"

I looked into a face that was all smiles and freckles.

"The pits," I said.

"Take heart. The higher the score, the more room for improvement."

"Hardly my intention to leave so much room for improvement."

"From one who's been there, the biggest kick of all is dropping your score."

Beefy arms propelled me outside. "How about telling me all about it—say, like next Saturday night."

"Saturday—I—I—"

Saturday, June 30, my fifteenth birthday. Aunt Lucy and Uncle Robb were coming in from Shenfield. Should I ask Danny for dinner too? But Mimi would be there, putting on her act.

"What time did you have in mind?" I asked warily.

"You name it."

"Eight thirty?" Surely by then Mimi would be gone.

"Look for me," he said.

Mom brought in the beautiful birthday cake and everyone sang, "Happy Birthday, dear Kate," Daddy and Uncle Robb in a booming bass, Mimi's voice sweet as wind chimes, and Aunt Lucy enthusiastically loud and off key.

"Blow out the candles, dear." Mom set the cake down in front of me.

"Not until you make a wish!" Mimi cried. She loved parties and her sparkle kept her in the spotlight.

I pushed back my chair and stood up. Somehow the whole ritual seemed childish, a hangover from Santa Claus days.

"Hurry," Mom said, "or we'll have waxed icing."

Fifteen small candles circled the taller center candle, the one to grow on. I shut my eyes and made a wish and blew. The small candles spluttered out, but the tall middle one burned on.

"It would be the one to grow on!"

"There are many ways to grow." Aunt Lucy laughed merrily. I liked Aunt Lucy the best of any of my aunts. She was a bouncy brunette who wrote the popular column "People and Places" for the weekly Shenfield paper. "You can grow up or out, or you can grow to be a better person." She gave me a wink. "Or a better golfer."

"That's for me." I made a great show of blowing out the last candle, then I sat down.

"And how's the golf?" Aunt Lucy said.

"Disaster."

"Come now," Aunt Lucy scoffed. "Nothing ever again will seem quite so disastrous as it does at your age." She leaned forward, eyes gleaming. "Actually, Kate, you're lucky to be starting golf now. It's too late for me."

Fifteen. Next summer I'd be sixteen, and there'd be no free clinics, no Bix to work with me. Bix had predicted that Lora would be a winner this year. Could I accomplish in one summer what had taken Lora seven? Absently I cut the cake and passed the slices around the table. My eyes sought out Aunt Lucy.

"It's never too late to play golf for the fun of it," I said, "and I bet if you tried the game, you'd love it just like I do. But suppose you hope to play tournament golf—even fifteen might be too late to start."

"Now I'm with it!" Aunt Lucy gave a vigorous nod. "I figured you'd taken up golf for kicks, something to do over vacation. But championship golf is something else altogether."

Mimi jangled the charms on her bracelet. "I just don't know why people get so hyped up over hitting an eensy-weensy ball. The only kind of ball I like is the kind with a thirty-piece band."

Uncle Robb laughed appreciatively, and Aunt Lucy went right on talking. "A few golfing greats began late. Babe Zaharias took up golf after she'd tried every other sport. But from what I've been reading—and I've been reading up a storm ever since I was assigned to cover the U.S. Girls' Junior Championship when it comes to Shenfield this summer—I'd have to say that the crop of champions gets better, and yes, younger, year by year. There's a cute thing, only eleven, coming from Biloxi to compete, and the defending champ, Meg Winchester, is only seventeen and is the odds-on favorite to win again this year."

I remembered seeing something about the Junior Championship in the sports section, but at the time I wasn't into golf myself, so the details hadn't registered.

But Aunt Lucy was up on everything. "Mark it down, sweetie," she said to me. "The first week in August. Two days of qualifying rounds and four days of play. It gets more exciting each day. We want you to come out and spend the weekend with us. Then you can see the wrap-up."

"Oh, Aunt Lucy."

"Hopefully the editor will give me a press

pass, but if not Uncle Robb will buy tickets for both of us, won't you?"

"Anything you say, dear." Uncle Robb pushed his plate aside, smiling at Mother. "Best cake I've ever had. If only I could get that restless wife of mine to stay home and bake!" But he looked at her adoringly.

"Yah-yah!" Aunt Lucy returned the adoring gaze. "If you dined on such caloric fare every night, you'd burst your seams! You wouldn't want that to happen, now would you?"

Uncle Robb jumped a little. "I thought I saw faces at the window."

It had to be Charles and Cecil. I cracked open the patio door and the boys skittered into the dining room.

"Well, well." Uncle Robb tipped back his chair. "And who are you?"

The boys eyed Uncle Robb coldly and Charles said, "You don't belong here."

"Oh, yes, he does," I said. "He's my uncle and he came all the way from Shenfield for my birthday dinner."

"You should have asked us, not him."

"This party is for grown-ups," I said, "but if you'll go outside, I'll bring you a piece of birthday cake."

"We eat here." Cecil swung a wooden sword and almost lopped off Uncle Robb's ear.

"Out!" I said, pushing the two of them through the door.

"I usta think you was nice," Charles said, "but you're mean just like my mother."

"Flattery will get you no place," I said.

I gave each of them a paper plate with a slice of cake and a plastic fork. They ignored the fork and attacked the cake with hands that hadn't seen soap in a week. I wondered how many pounds of dirt coated their stomachs.

"If you ask me," Mimi said, "families with little boys should have to have special building permits."

"Little boys grow into big boys," Mother said judiciously. "They cut lawns and carry in groceries." The doorbell rang, and when Mimi jumped up Mom added, "And take pretty girls out to parties."

7

Mimi and Ron left arm in arm. At least I didn't lose my cool. I wouldn't want someone as independent as Aunt Lucy to know that I'd knocked myself out for Ron—and he'd dumped me.

I excused myself and went to my room. I stripped off my new birthday dress and pulled on jeans. I caught a glimpse of myself in the mirror and was pleasantly surprised. The sun had given my hair—Mimi called my hair mud colored—some gold highlights, and already I had a deep, if somewhat uneven, tan. The hand where I wore a golf glove was still stark white, and my ankles where my socks had been looked funny too, but if Danny noticed at all, he'd consider the white stripes the merit badges of a golfer.

A station wagon stopped out front. Danny. I tucked the score card he'd asked me to bring into a back pocket and answered the door. A face of shining freckles greeted me. Danny was not Ron, but at least he had asked me out instead of my asking him and I was glad of that.

"Come in," I said. But he stood on the porch, shifting his weight, staring at his feet. I held open the screen. No waves of electricity jumped between us. My heart didn't skyrocket. On the other hand, it didn't sink. Danny had a comforting effect on me. I felt *at home* with him. Yet unless we were talking golf, he seemed awfully shy, and I found myself trying to put him at ease.

"Someone I want you to meet." I led the way into the dining room and introduced him to my parents and Uncle Robb, adding, "And this is Aunt Lucy. She's invited me to the U.S. Girls' Championship."

"Swan Lake's a tough course," Danny said.

So he knew all about it!

Aunt Lucy smiled. "It does look like a challenge. We live in Shenfield and the course is halfway between my house and my job so I drive past it nearly every day."

"Would you like a slice of Kate's birthday cake?" Mother said.

Danny looked at me. "You didn't tell me it was your birthday."

"I didn't want to make a thing of it."

"Well, I could have brought you a golf ball or something."

"A shag ball?"

Danny grinned. "One of my better shag balls."

"Is this too much?" Mother said.

"It should be—I just finished off half a pie—but thanks, I'd like to try the birthday cake."

Danny gulped the cake and we said goodbye and drove off.

"Where to?" Danny said.

"You name it."

"Well, there's a horror movie and there's the Poison Penguin—"

"Oh, it's such a fabulous night, I'd hate to go inside." Actually I hated horror shows and you had to rob the bank to go to the Penguin, and since our bet had only been a quarter—

"Hoping you'd say that." Danny looked relieved.

Like a homing pigeon, Danny drove to Willow Tree Park. Only tonight was so different from the night I'd come here alone. As we walked along the path side by side, I told him about the evening I'd just happened into the park, and just happened to see some golfers, and just happened into the clubhouse to inquire about golf. Of course I didn't mention Mimi or Ron or the Jamboree I'd never been invited to.

"Do you believe in fate?" I said.

"I'm beginning to."

"That night was a turning point. Golf made all the difference."

"Yeah," Danny said as we walked toward the pond. "It has for me too. I'm in line for a golf scholarship at State, and that's the only way I'll ever see a campus, believe me."

"And I'd be sitting home right now," I said, "all day every day."

"Did you remember the card?" Danny asked.

I reached into my pocket.

"For lack of a park bench, could I persuade you—" Danny hoisted me up onto a wide flat branch of a willow tree. My feet dangled only inches above the water. Willow tendrils hung all around us like the bars on a cage giving me a feeling of privacy.

"They forgot one thing," Danny said. "Seat belts. If you fall in, don't expect me to be a hero and rescue you."

"Snake country, if you ask me." I sniffed the brackish water.

"Now for that score card."

"Take it and tear it up. I don't want to go over that round ever again, blow after missed blow."

Danny studied the card while I listened to the shrilling of insects in the grass along the bank.

"You've already told me about the first hole, but whatever happened on seven? You piled up fifteen strokes."

"A hole of horrors," I conceded. "The rough, the trap, the trees, and some more rough. I just couldn't make it back to the fairway." I sighed. "Sometimes I think that's my game plan for life. In the rough."

Danny dismissed that with a wave of his hand. "Sooner or later everyone gets in the rough. The problem is how to get out." He looked at me. "Do you remember which side you were on?"

"Oh, yes. Right the whole way."

"It hardly takes a genius," Danny said, "to figure out that you're slicing. A common complaint."

"If only I could be like Lora—straight all the way."

"Lora's probably wishing she had your big swing."

"But she almost broke ninety!"

"Sure. But when you've had all the experience she has, you'll be able to break eighty, maybe someday seventy, and I doubt if she'll ever be able to do that."

"Dreams are cheap," I said, remembering the high hopes I'd had at the beginning of that first round.

"I'm quoting Bix and he's not given to dreaming. Now about that slice. Try to work it out yourself, but if you're still in trouble, see the boss."

Suddenly it was dark. Stars glimmered in the night sky. Music flooded the air. "The summer symphony!" I swayed to the strains of *Die Fledermaus*. "What are we waiting for?"

Danny lifted me down from the willow tree. I half walked and half waltzed toward the sound of the music. Danny was having none of that. He plodded along behind me. The orchestra was set up in an illuminated band shell at the far end of the park. We sat down on an empty bench at the back. A mounted policeman rode by, and when his handsome horse lifted his hooves in time to the music, we both laughed.

The concert ended and I clapped loudly, hoping for an encore, but the musicians took a bow and, carrying their instruments, shuffled down the steps of the band shell to the waiting bus.

"Hungry?" Danny stood up and stretched.

"No way. I'm up to here in birthday cake." No sooner were the words out than I realized I'd said the wrong thing. "But that doesn't mean I won't go along with you—that is, if you could possibly eat again."

He grinned. "Sure, I can always eat."

We stopped by The Shack on the edge of town. The place was jumping, but we finally managed to crowd into a booth with a couple of kids from North that I'd seen hanging out with Mimi. It was so noisy Danny and I didn't even try to talk but we smiled at each other and made silly signs with our fingers.

The pizza arrived at last. Plate size. He attacked it with relish. The only trouble was that he got all tangled up in the cheese that stretched and snapped like rubber bands.

"What a mess." I made a face.

"Simply super." I read his lips as he finished off the last morsel.

Glancing at the big clock above the counter, I screamed above the din, "I'd better get back." If we'd gone to the movie, I figured we'd be getting out just about now.

Danny parked the wagon in front of our house, switching off the lights as if he expected to stay awhile. He walked me up to the door, but I wasn't about to invite him in. But when his big hand squeezed mine and he said, "I hope it's been a happy birthday, Kate," I relented.

"Would you like to come in for a few minutes?"

He beamed. "I'd like that."

I stepped into the hall and froze in my tracks. Mimi was rattling around upstairs.

"Shh!" I put my finger to my lips and mouthed the words, "Follow me." I tiptoed along the hall and ducked into the den, holding the door open for Danny. Once he was safely inside, I eased the door shut and switched the FM station on low. The music was soft and soothing and a cover-up for our voices.

"Help yourself," I said in a muted voice, and gestured toward the couch.

Danny lowered himself to the couch and sat gingerly on the edge of a cushion. "Hey, if my being here is getting you in trouble with your parents—"

"Not my parents. It's my sister."

"And what's she got on you?" Danny looked amused as he settled back.

"That's a good question." I fiddled with the tuner, my back to Danny. Of course, I couldn't come out with what I was really thinking—that foxy Mimi would be down in no time if she knew Danny was in the den and Danny would go the way of all the boys I'd ever known—right out of my life. I didn't need that. Especially on my birthday.

"Younger sisters can be very nosy," I said.

"I've got one of those." Danny forced his voice up into a falsetto. "Oh, Moth-er," he croaked, "just look at what I found in Danny's bureau drawer."

I cracked up. "I bet you could wring her little neck."

"Happily. But I'm not allowed to touch so much as a pigtail."

I felt sort of good about Danny telling me about his sister. That's one thing we had in common. Younger sisters that drove us up the wall.

Danny sang along with the vocalist who was doing a Cole Porter oldie.

"I like your voice," I said. "I bet you sang in the choir."

"Forever. Then my voice changed."

"It's still a nice voice," I said, which was true, but it was also true that it didn't have the rich overtones that made Ron's speaking voice so unique.

Stop thinking of Ron. I dug my nails into the palm of my hand as a reminder. Tucking my feet up under me, I turned my full attention to Danny.

"There are just two girls in our family," I said, trying to draw him out. "And we're not anything alike."

"I have two sisters that are okay and then there's little Miss Tattle Tale."

"Can't win them all." I shrugged. "I take it you're the only boy."

Danny flinched, and he's not scared of anything. I had a funny feeling.

"Something wrong?"

A shadow passed over his eyes, darkening them, and his tanned skin seemed to pale, making the freckles stand out.

"I'm the oldest," Danny said with great restraint. "Actually I'm the man of the family. Dad was killed. He was a construction worker and a wet concrete wall collapsed on him and he was trapped."

I shuddered. "How horrible."

"Yes." He sat silently and I knew he was thinking of his father and my hand reached out and even that small gesture seemed to comfort him. He straightened. "I'm lucky about one thing. Uncle Alex has taken me under his wing. My grades are okay but not really hot, but Uncle Alex thinks my golf is good enough so I can get a golf scholarship, and believe me that's the only way I'll see college. Mom works in a bank, but as she says, she doesn't manufacture the green stuff, she just counts it. Here's the choice she gives us—sink or swim."

"I can tell you right now—you'll swim."

"Of course, everyone hopes for the golf circuit, but if I don't make it—and not many do—I'd like to be a teaching pro, right here with Uncle Alex. Or maybe run my own driving range."

"I envy you. You've got it all together. Just what you want to do."

"Don't you?"

"Are you kidding?" I could feel Danny's eyes on me, and I turned my head away so he couldn't read my see-through face. Oh, yes, I'd believed Ron when he'd told me we should go to the same college. Partners. And try as I would—and I have tried—I still haven't been able to turn off all those lovely dreams: Ron and I walking hand in hand across campus; Ron and I studying in the deep cool recesses of the library, sneaking off to the stacks; Ron paddling a canoe into the sunset as I lie supine across the thwarts—I closed my eyes and clasped my hands. If only I could erase those hurting dreams! If only— I leaped up from the couch, startled.

"Did you hear that?" I pointed to the ceiling and trembled. "The natives are getting restless and I have to throw you out." Now it was my turn to give his hand a squeeze. "And thanks, Danny—it's the most beautiful birthday I ever remember."

"You mean that?" He smiled.

"I mean it, and we'll see each other real soon—like Monday."

He gave me a kiss on the cheek, which was sweet of him. I had told him the truth. It had been a beautiful birthday and Danny, I decided, was a right-enough guy.

I turned off the FM and plumped up the cushions and rid the den of any evidence of a visitor before I went upstairs. I wasn't in the least surprised when Mimi called out from her room.

"Where've you been, Kate?"

"To a concert at Willow Tree Park and then The Shack."

"Yuck!" Mimi propped herself up on a dimpled elbow and made a face.

"And you?" I asked politely.

"Ron took me to the Poison Penguin." Mimi babbled on. "Was it ever neat. Green sandwiches and a drink called Hemlock and a groovy guy on the drums."

I played it cool. "We talked about there," I said with a little shrug, "but decided against it."

Mimi bounced upright. "You had the chance to go to the Penguin and you went to a dumb concert?"

"That's right," I said sweetly, moving toward the door. "We just missed you."

In a spirit of thankfulness I fed Samson and Delilah an extra fish flake.

8

My first tournament. I poured myself a double slug of orange juice, extra vitamins to keep my energy up, and set the timer for a three-minute egg.

In no time at all Bix had cured my slice, but when I asked him how to be a successful competitor, he said, "That's something you must find out for yourself. Some players do the impossible under pressure, others blow. But I'll tell you one thing, Kate—winning and losing start right here." He tapped his head. "Think positively," he said. "Think win."

I lifted the egg out of the pan and cracked it

on the edge of my cup. I tried to psych myself up.

"Think pos-i-tive-ly." I took a deep breath. "Think—"

"Aaargggh!" I jumped at the unexpected sound of Mimi's voice. "Whatcha got, a case of early senility, muttering to yourself?"

I shot her a drop-dead glance. "I'll try to kick the habit."

Mimi yawned and I thought, She's even pretty when she yawns.

"How come you're up so early?" I said.

"Hardly my idea. Ron said if we were going to make his cottage for lunch—"

"All that way for lunch?"

"Why not? Not much action around here."

"For me there's plenty. I'm playing in a real tournament. Cross your fingers and cross your toes that my ball stays straight."

Mimi yawned again and twisted her long hair into a topknot. "Do you like the new way I'm wearing it?"

"I hadn't noticed."

"You haven't registered on a thing all summer."

"Oh, haven't I!" I broke off. I couldn't afford to let Mimi stir me up. I couldn't afford to be tense and uptight for the match. I ate silently and left for the park.

"I'm early," I told Bix as I checked in.

"Good!" Bix leaped up and rushed me out to the first tee. "One of the girls canceled, and I need a substitute right now. The others have hit, so go right ahead, Kate." He made hasty introductions. "The McNab sisters, Martha and Mary, and I believe you know Sharkey Jones."

I dropped back. So I'd arrived early only to find myself in the same foursome with Sharkey!

"I haven't caught my breath yet," I said.

Bix glared, and I knew even that little attempt to postpone the inevitable had annoyed him. But when I stepped up to the tee, he lowered his voice. "Don't let anything distract you. Keep your mind on your own game."

I realized Bix was trying to tell me something important, something just as important as the correct stance and the proper swing. I willed my taut muscles to relax. The day was to my liking—on the cool side with plump clouds bouncing along the horizon like boats on a spinnaker run. There was the song of birds and voices.

I set myself up over the ball and all talking ceased. There was a feeling of expectancy. I coiled up and slammed the drive.

"Geez," Sharkey said, "a bruiser."

"Straight." I sighed with relief.

Bix waved us off. "When you're through, bring your score cards to me."

From the beginning the McNab sisters were outclassed. They advanced the ball a bit at a time, but this did not seem to bother them. "At least I didn't whiff," one consoled the other.

My drive was big—but Sharkey's was bigger.

"Super shot," I said politely.

"I don't hold back." Sharkey bared her teeth. "I play to win."

"Me too."

"You?" Sharkey guffawed. "I know a softie when I see one."

I bristled, but I didn't say anything. Someday I'd show Sharkey.

Sharkey's ball had rolled into a hole. I was glad I didn't have to cope with a buried lie, and I wondered what she was going to do about it.

She studied the lie with beady eyes, then she reared back, slashing down on the ball viciously. Not surprising that it hooked and ended up behind a tree. In trouble again.

Still, she managed some sort of shot that sent the ball bulleting through a peephole in the foliage, landing it on the green. Nothing seemed to stop her—a crazy swing, a bad lie, or even a big tree.

I felt little drops of perspiration break out along my upper lip. I'd hoped for a long straight ball. I had it. But it wasn't good enough.

Sharkey whistled happily as she crossed over to the next tee. "How did you like them apples?"

I didn't answer. I couldn't. Only one hole and I had the shakes.

"You're new at the game." Sharkey gave me a condescending look. "I can show you a thing or two. If you want to learn how it's done, just watch me."

An alert beeped in my brain. Sharkey was calling attention to her swing, a strange unorthodox swing that worked for her, but wasn't meant for me. Bix had warned me. Lora too.

"You do your own thing." I made an effort to pull myself together. "And I'll do mine."

I turned my back. So Sharkey had been lucky getting through that small opening in the tree! No one could luck out forever.

The match seesawed back and forth, with the McNab sisters far behind. But I was the one on top going into the sixteenth hole. All I had to do was hang on to my lead for a win.

"Really something," Sharkey remarked as I

stepped up to address the ball, "how you stay on the fairway at all with that overswing of yours. If I overswung like that, I'd be right in the middle of them there trees." She pointed out the clump of trees on the right.

Overswing. I didn't like the sound of it. The last time I'd played this hole I had tangled with those trees and it had cost me two strokes to get out. I couldn't afford that sort of trouble. I gave the ball a cautious punch. It didn't go far, but at least it wasn't under a tree.

When at last I sank my final putt, I felt a little dizzy, as if something had happened to my equilibrium, but I wasn't sure what. I made my way into the clubhouse with my score card curled in my hot hand. I turned it in to Bix.

"Congratulations," he said. "A very fine round—your best to date. A tie with Sharkey. Commendable."

"But I was leading—"

The counter was crowded. "I want to hear all about it," Bix said, "but some other time."

Suddenly I felt very tired. The thought of biking home seemed too much. I sat down on a bench and was glad when Danny came over and sat down beside me.

"Bix told me you had a great round today, but you hardly seem to be celebrating."

"Everything was going for me—my woods, my irons, and my putter was hot. I couldn't ask for anything more. I kept gaining on Sharkey and actually had a lead going into the sixteenth."

"Then you sliced," Danny said. "I know all about that clump of tree."

"No, I was straight all the way in. But from the moment Sharkey called attention to my overswing—"

"There's no such thing as an overswing." Danny drummed his fingers on the bench and looked at me quizzically. "Sure, a big swing can go off more easily than a short swing, but so long as you don't drop your club head at the top—"

"So Sharkey took me," I said.

"The name of that game is gamesmanship, and in the course of tournament play you're bound to run into a few con artists. They wouldn't dream of actually cheating, but they think it's all part of the game to rattle the opponent."

Now I was able to laugh at myself. "I was smart enough not to look at Sharkey, but I wasn't smart enough not to listen to her. I'm so easily distracted I should wear earplugs."

"Not a bad idea at that." Danny nodded and stood up. "C'mon, Kate—we'll go over to The Shack for a hamburger."

"I couldn't eat a thing." My stomach felt hollow but not hungry.

Danny stretched out his hands and lifted me up. "Then you can watch me eat," he said.

"Gross."

"This time I'll go easy on the onions."

"Now that's the supreme sacrifice." I turned. "Give me a sec to wash up and I'll be with you."

I did a quick mirror check and practically flipped. I was a disaster. Hair on end, perspiration pouring down my cheeks, and pale cracked lips. I looked so grungy I began to laugh and the girl standing next to me glared. But I couldn't help myself. Imagine a guy being so unconscious that he'd ask out such a witch!

The soap and water felt good. I untangled my hair with my pocket comb and put on lipstick. I was now the picture of health—if not beauty.

Lora was talking to Danny when I returned. Her face was fire red, the kind of color scheme brought on by heat and exertion.

"I take it you just finished your match." Seeing the sparkle in her eyes, I added, "And you did a great job."

"It's my birthday irons. I just love them."

"And every year your swing gets better and better," Danny said.

"Oh, you've been watching me?" Lora looked pleased and a little flustered.

My heart went out to her. That's the way it had been with Ron. Any little crumb of kindness set me up.

"And how did you make out with Sharkey?" Lora asked.

"For fifteen holes I handled her—then she handled me."

Lora's lips thinned. "If one trick doesn't work, she tries another."

"I believe anything." I felt a pang. It didn't seem right that I was going off to lunch with Danny and cutting Lora out. "We're on our way to The Shack," I said. "Why don't you join us?"

"Gee, that's nice of you. But I promised Mom I'd come home after golf to help out. Some other time?" She looked at Danny hopefully, but Danny was more than a little dense, so I filled in. "You bet."

The Shack wasn't as busy as sometimes. Only a few bikes in the stand and the parking lot was almost empty.

"Where is everyone?" I asked as Danny parked the wagon in a slot near the door.

"It's still early. Not even noon."

"Really?" My inner time clock was all screwed up. I felt as if the day should be over. But then I'm not used to getting up at dawn, and the match with Sharkey had been more taxing than a day in the salt mines.

I opened the car door and stepped out. The geraniums in the long window box bloomed in pink and white clusters. I was glad now that Danny had persuaded me to come. I needed to unwind.

With just a few people inside, The Shack looked bigger—cleaner too—without the usual litter of paper, food, and drink. Hamburgers sizzled on the grill behind the counter and smelled so good I knew my appetite had returned.

"Where do you want to sit?" Danny asked.

"Maybe we should take a table for two in case the place fills up."

"That's my Kate. Always thinking of someone else."

I smiled. "Okay if I change my mind? I could use a burger with the works."

"A little darling after me own heart."

Danny touched his heart, letting his hand slide to his stomach, and I giggled.

He leaned on the counter waiting for the order while I zigzagged my way toward the small tables at the back. A hand reached out from a booth and grabbed me. I jumped. A bracelet jangled.

"Mimi!" I cried. "What are you doing here?"

She laughed her tinkling laugh, obviously enjoying my consternation. She looked cool as a blue icicle in a shift that matched her eyes.

I persisted. "When I left this morning, you were on your way to Ron's cottage for lunch."

"Well, I admit it's the pits." She pursed her lips. "But Ron's car wouldn't start and without wheels the best laid plans—"

"Where is Ron now?" I could feel my nerves vibrate.

"He's over in Bob's Garage riding herd on the mechanics."

"You mean you're here all by yourself?"

"Not for long. Ron told me to meet him here at noon. I got Mom to drop me off on her way to the Hair House."

Ron would be here any minute. Why should I care? Ron was nothing to me. Why, then, did my heart go thump? Why, then, did my knees that had held me up through eighteen holes of golf start to wobble? Why couldn't I forget the guy?

"And who are you with?" Mimi watched me closely.

"Danny."

She leaned out of the booth and looked toward the counter. "The big guy?"

"The one."

"Mmm." Mimi licked her lips. "Such beautiful biceps."

"What a crazy thing to say."

"Haven't you noticed?"

"Danny's strong. I'll give you that. He can whack a ball right out of sight."

"That's one thing about being tiny," Mimi said with a flick of her lashes. "I make strong men feel even stronger."

I gnashed my teeth. "You've got Ron to yourself for lunch. Isn't that enough for you?"

"Now, Kate—"

I didn't answer. I slipped into a booth that looked out on the street. I began to shake. I had to get out of here before I heard Ron's silver-toned voice and looked into his luminous, laughing eyes.

"Hey, Kate," Danny said, handing me a plate, "what are you doing in a booth after telling me good guys sit at a table for two?"

"I have to look out the window."

"Why so?"

"Trust me."

He shrugged. "I trust you but that doesn't mean I understand you."

"How could you?" I sighed. "I don't understand myself."

"Sorry about the Pepsi," he said. "It spilled." He wiped off the outside of the plastic cup before setting it down in front of me. "You won't believe this—but on my way over some jerk grabbed me by the pant legs."

I straightened. Warning signals bleeped. "Who?" I said.

"A hand shot out of a booth, and I guess it was a girl, but I was carrying all this stuff and I didn't have a chance to look."

My fingers flew to my throat and I must have turned pale. At least Danny seemed concerned about me. "Is it someone you know?"

"Someone I wish I didn't know." I cleared my throat and tried not to sound overly inquisitive. "But what did you do when the hand—"

"I made snarling noises and the hand let go."

"Beautiful," I said, diving into the hamburger. It was delicious—all slathered with catsup and mustard and pickle relish and onions.

I heard the squealing tires before I saw the car. Ron!

"I've got to go." I grasped the edge of the table and slid out of the booth. I ran headlong out the door and didn't stop running until I was safe in Danny's wagon. With a sigh of relief, I curled up into a ball on the floor.

Great guy, Danny. He didn't rave or rant or even ask questions. He just brought me the rest of my hamburger wrapped in a paper napkin.

"Thanks," I said.

9

Mr. Dubois plodded slowly down the row of tomatoes, shoulders hunched, hoe dragging. He stooped to tie up a top-heavy plant, but his hands fumbled and the plant sagged back to the ground.

I threw aside my sand wedge. "Are you all right?" I said.

Mr. Dubois let out a creaky sigh. "Angel's feeling poorly. All tuckered out. She gets up a bit, then goes back to bed." He shook his head. "Not like her."

"It really isn't," I said. A series of pictures ran through my mind: Mrs. Dubois weeding; Mrs. Dubois stacking sparkling jars of peaches and pears, watermelon pickle, and cranberry relish on the pantry shelves; Mrs. Dubois filling the cookie jar with moons and stars, with shortbread squares and gingerbread men, so much tastier than what I once called the "store-boughten" kind.

"Doc came last night." Mr. Dubois wheezed. "Tomorrow she goes to the hospital for tests." He rubbed his hand on his stubbled chin. "I'll have to drag her. She's fighting it."

"Let me know how things go."

"I'll do that." Mr. Dubois shuffled toward the house and I started back toward the sand trap. But I didn't feel like practicing. I ran after him.

"Let me cook dinner for you tonight," I said in a rush of words.

"Not necessary." His eyebrows knit together in a severe line.

"I'd have fun doing it. And Mrs. Dubois can stay in bed and you won't have to fuss over the stove." I added, "Of course, you've got to understand I'm a lousy cook."

Mr. Dubois smiled a little. "Mighty nice of you, Kate. We eat simple, you know."

"It'll be simple, all right," I said. "Look for me about six."

Cook dinner? What did I know about cooking anything except chocolate chip cookies? I sat on the kitchen stool riffling through Mom's cookbooks. There were volumes on international cooking, casserole cooking, cookbooks edited by newspapers and magazines, cookbooks on the joy of cooking and others for those who hated to cook. There were more pages in these books than in all the textbooks I had read last year in school.

"I never dreamed it was such a problem getting dinner on the table," I told Mother.

"Don't let all those recipes scare you, dear. I love to read recipes and it's a challenge trying something new now and then." She peeked over my shoulder. "Is there some special reason why you want to attempt Oysters Rockefeller?"

"I haven't read beyond the appetizers yet." I told Mom that Mrs. Dubois was sick and I'd promised to take dinner next door.

Mom gave me a quick hug. "I'm so glad you offered, Kate. They've been the friendliest neighbors, sending over fresh vegetables year after year."

"And they've let me dig up their yard with traps and things."

"But remember, Kate, for someone sick choose things that are easy to digest. Forget the

fancy receipes with the maraschino cherries.
Forget the rich foods and the fried foods."

"So what's left?"

"Most everything." Mom added, "We can
spare chicken from our dinner tonight. Make a
jello mold so it will be firm by dinner. And I
have a recipe for Perfect Custard."

"How do you know it's perfect until you
make it?"

"Aunt Stella experimented for years and
came up with a custard that won't collapse
under any circumstances."

"She doesn't know me."

Mom took a card from her recipe file. "Very
nutritious," she said.

I scurried around the kitchen in a fever of
activity. Bowls and beaters, eggs, and it took a
while to find the nutmeg.

Mimi, barefoot and pajama clad, padded into
the kitchen.

"Some goodie for breakfast?"

"I'm working on dinner."

Sleepy eyes brightened. "Oh, company?"

"Wrong again. I'm taking dinner next door.
Mrs. Dubois is sick."

"That's too bad." Mimi yawned. "But, of
course, she is an old lady."

"She's my friend," I said a bit savagely as I beat the yolks into a yellow froth, a shade more vivid than Mimi's silken hair.

The phone rang and Mimi scurried toward the TV room. She came back frowning.

"It's for you."

Aunt Lucy's voice came through loud and clear. "Everything's set, Kate. I have the tickets for the Girls' Championship and something new has been added. The Shenfield Press and Swan Lake Country Club are co-sponsoring a dinner for the players right after Saturday's final match."

"Oh, Aunt Lucy, a chance to meet the players!"

"So plan to stay through Sunday." Aunt Lucy raised her voice. "Tell me, how's *your* golf going?"

"Rolling along. I've dropped my score each round and Bix says if I keep it up I'll get to play in the city championship at Metro Park."

"City championship?" Aunt Lucy interjected in her sharp reporter voice. "Your first year of golf. Fantastic!"

"Well, Bix will let me know tomorrow."

"If you've come this far," Aunt Lucy said, "there'll be no stopping you."

"I can think of a lot of things that might stand in my way," I said. Still, when I returned to the kitchen I felt pumped up.

"And Mom accuses me of tying up the phone," Mimi said crossly.

"Aunt Lucy and I had to make plans for the Junior Championship."

"Who cares?"

"And plans for the dinner at the club after the tournament."

"Dinner?" Mimi took a step toward me. "Did she say anything about me joining her for dinner? Ron could drive me out."

"No, she didn't mention you."

"But I'm her niece too."

"The dinner's for golfers," I said, "and, well, golf is not your thing."

"How did it go today?" Bix asked.

"I was only in the rough a couple of times, and that makes all the difference." I set my clubs in the rack and entered my score in the handicap book.

Bix checked the book. "That settles it. You'll be playing in the city championship tomorrow. Danny will pick you up at eight."

My pulse gave an excited leap. "Thanks, Bix."

"Thank yourself." He grinned and I felt really good.

"You'll never know how much you've helped me."

"That's what a pro is for. But only you can drive that ball or drop that putt and keep your cool when the heat's on."

In a daze of happiness I headed for the practice range. What would Metro Park be like? Lora had played it time and again. She said that the sand in the traps was fluffier than the sand at Willow Tree Park and that a stream cut through Metro and if a ball fell in the water there was a penalty.

Water. I knew nothing about water hazards. Suppose all of my balls dropped into the water and were carried downstream by the current. What then? My head began to spin. With faltering steps I walked back to the clubhouse.

"I don't feel well," I told Bix. "I'm coming down with something terrible. I'm telling you now so you can get a substitute right away."

Bix laughed and I thought, Crazy!

"Headache?" he asked.

"Yes."

"Dizzy?"

"You bet."

"Rumbling stomach?"

I nodded. "Is there a bug going around?"

"A golf bug," Bix said. "It's a common complaint on the circuit. I've had the symptoms many times myself. But for what it's worth, the symptoms pass once you're under way."

So Bix didn't think I was sick at all! Nevertheless, I didn't feel up to playing tomorrow.

"I can't hack it," I said. "I'm too new at the game."

"Ten years from now you'd be telling me the same thing. If you want to improve, you've got to move on. New courses, new situations, new opponents. That's what you need to make the big time."

So that was it! Win or lose, playing in the city tournament was an opportunity.

"Naturally I want to be in on the action." I tried to lay it all out so Bix would understand. "It's just that I'm not seasoned like Lora and—" I broke off, gagging over the name Sharkey. But, of course, Sharkey was in there. She and Lora had the lowest handicaps of all the girls. "But, Bix, suppose I fall apart. Suppose I disgrace you."

"You won't." Bix acted as if the matter were settled. He handed me a new ball. "Take it. It may bring you luck. Go home. Eat a big dinner, a light breakfast, and above all get plenty of sleep. Get your clubs in order. Give yourself every break. From then on, don't worry. Open up with that big swing and let her rip."

Bix's pep talk had a bracing effect. I went home and treated myself to a nap—something I never did unless I was running a raging fever. Mom even waited dinner for me, and when I sat down she told me how much Mrs. Dubois had appreciated the Perfect Custard.

Dad leaned across the table and patted my hand. It had been years since he'd done that.

"Hope I don't have to get sick before you make a custard for me."

"For you, I'll make one with caramel icing." I smiled. I turned to Mom. "Any news of Mrs. Dubois?"

"As I understand it, they won't know the results of the tests for several days."

The doorbell rang and Dad said, "Can't we even finish our dinner—"

Mimi jumped up. "Don't hang it on me. We had to wait around for Kate."

Ron's arrival signaled everyone's departure. Mom and Dad took their coffee in the TV room and I exited to the kitchen, where I made short work of the dishes. Then I tackled my clubs, scrubbing away the slivers of grass that had wormed their way into the laminated faces of the woods and into the grooves of the irons. I even touched up the mahogany heads with furniture polish.

Music drifted through the closed kitchen door. I pictured the scene in the living room— Ron seated in Dad's leather chair and Mimi on the footstool, strumming her guitar. Ron sang—that gorgeous voice—and I hummed, for the moment forgetting I was alone in the kitchen, left out. The music stopped.

"What'll it be, pet?" Ron said. "Pepsi or Pepsi?"

"You guessed right the first time." Mimi's silver laugh.

"Try to live without me while I'm gone," Ron said. The kitchen door creaked open. My back stiffened.

"Hello there," Ron said, leaning over my shoulder. He was so close I could feel the warmth of his body, smell the after-shave lotion.

"Hello yourself."

"Whatcha doing?"

"Listening to you and Mimi make music."

"Not that. Why all the golf clubs in the sink?"

"Where else would you wash them?"

"Whoever heard of giving golf clubs such TLC?"

"Orders from the boss," I said. "He told me to make everything shipshape for the city championship tomorrow."

"City championship?" Ron's eyes flashed. Instead of looking through me as he'd done ever since he'd discovered Mimi, he actually seemed to be seeing me as a real live someone who mattered. "I'd be a louse and a liar if I didn't tell you I'm impressed."

"It's just for Juniors. No big thing."

"You bet it's big. I read about it in the Sports Section. Only the best in the city qualify, and you're just a beginner." He ran his fingers along the shaft of a club. "With a start like this, I expect you'll make the Golfing Hall of Fame one of these days."

"Don't bet on it," I said curtly, but at the moment anything seemed possible. Ron was acting excited about the match, excited about me. He pressed his hand into the small of my back and I felt little shock waves shoot up my spine.

The kitchen door burst open. Mimi leaned against it, her cheeks flaming.

"How can you take so long?"

"I get distracted easily," Ron said, and I envied the smooth way he handled things.

"Doesn't it matter at all that I'm waiting?"

Ron didn't answer that. Instead he said, "Isn't it something that Kate's playing in the city championship?"

"I wouldn't know. How come you know so much?"

"Kate's the modest sort. I had to drag it out of her."

"Well, I'm not interested in golf and I never knew you were."

"Still, she should be congratulated."

"Congratulations," Mimi said sweetly, and left.

At the door, Ron saluted. "Win," he said.

That night I dreamed of Ron and I dreamed of victory.

10

Danny parked the wagon in the Metro lot and Lora and I jumped out. With an effortless touch, he pulled the heavy golf bags over the tailgate, propping them against the side of the car. He looked at his watch.

"Sorry to run, but—"

"That's what comes from being in the Championship Flight," Lora said. Her eyes glinted. "Luck all the way, Danny."

"Thanks and the same to both of you." He gave me a little nudge. "You can do it, Kate."

He slung his bag over his shoulder and took off at a trot. I started to follow him, but Lora tugged at my arm.

"Wait. Girls sign in this-a-way."

We followed the arrows posted on trees along a black-topped path. Arrow after arrow. My scalp prickled.

"Did you panic the first time you played Metro?" I asked.

"I was too young and too dumb," Lora said. "But so much is riding on today, I'm ready to jump out of my jeans."

"Not you," I said. "You're so steady Bix calls you 'old automatic,' a perfect ball time after time." I sighed. "Now my game's something else. First I have it, then I don't."

"You can't go wrong," Lora said. "If you do well, everyone'll think you're terrific. If you blow—so you lack experience."

But in my heart I knew that today was a crossroad—one way leading to the District and the golfing life and the other road taking me someplace else.

The path ended alongside a table set up in the shade of a beech tree. An official checked our handicaps and directed us to the tee. The wavering croak of a bullhorn drummed at my ears and I looked at Lora.

"Oh, that's just the starter announcing the next foursome. The foursome stands by, what's called 'on deck,' ready to tee off the minute the players ahead are out of range."

"I never dreamed any of this would be happening to little old me." I grimaced. "But I'd like it better if the starter whispered in my ear."

Lora laughed, then her face sobered. "Only hope I don't have a long wait."

She didn't, but I wasn't scheduled to go for some time. I stood on the sidelines among strangers, the bullhorn squawking every few minutes.

"Do I have to wait right here?" I asked nervously.

The starter shot me a sympathetic glance. "There's a practice green over by the caddy house. When you hear your name called, hurry back."

Dozens of boys and girls crowded around the practice green. Some were chipping from the fringe, others were putting. I dropped my golf bag among the other bags under a tree and, taking a putter, joined the group on the green. My first putt scooted so far beyond the cup, I was dumbfounded. I looked the green over more closely. It was clipped shorter than the greens at Willow Tree Park, so naturally the ball ran faster and farther, and that meant a more delicate touch. Lucky to find that out before my match started.

I lost track of time. It was a real shock hearing my name called. I grabbed my golf bag off the pile and ran up the path.

"I'm here," I said breathlessly. The starter handed me a score card and told me to keep my opponent's score and my opponent would keep mine. At the end of the match, each player would sign and attest her own score. Check and double check.

I glanced at the name on top of the card. Sharkey Jones.

A strangled sound erupted deep in my throat and exploded through clenched teeth.

"Is something wrong?" The starter eyed me curiously.

"No," I said hastily.

Danny had shown me how to handle Sharkey. Don't look at her. Don't listen to her.

"How's that overswing?" Sharkey asked, her lips curling ever so slightly.

"Fine, just fine." I smiled vaguely as if I hadn't quite heard. I introduced myself to the others in the foursome. Bubbles Bartowski looked more brash than bubbly with corkscrew curls, green eyelids, and silver lips. She could cope. But what about the little thing who said, "Just call me Missy." Easy pickings for Sharkey. Yet how could I say to someone I'd just met, "Watch out for Charlotte the Shark. She'll eat you up."

The bullhorn blared again, this time urging me to tee off. I placed the lucky ball Bix had given me on the tee. At that moment an orange-red butterfly brightly spotted with black and blue dots swooped down on top of my ball, wings spread, hovering. I gasped. No mistaking it. The butterfly was a Red Admiral and everyone knows Red Admirals bring luck. A good luck ball, and now a good luck butterfly! A double omen. That could mean only one thing. I was meant to beat Sharkey. Danny had said competition got his adrenaline up. I, too, could feel the juices flow. New power, new strength, new certainty.

The butterfly winged upward. I stepped up and cannonballed the lucky ball off into space.

From that moment on I could do no wrong. I seemed to have been given a bit extra of everything—especially extra luck. The bad shot I hit on number three struck a tree, but the ball ricocheted back on the fairway for an easy pitch.

Bubbles moaned, "You're killing us."

On the green Sharkey said, "I don't know how you putt so well the way you drag your putter."

I was on to Sharkey's little games. "Do me a favor and don't talk to me while I'm putting."

"That was a lousy remark," Bubbles hissed at Sharkey, and Sharkey dropped her head, subdued. But for how long?

We crossed over to play the back nine. The impossible continued to happen. The water hole. My ball bounced like a skipping stone across the stream, saving me from what looked like an almost certain penalty. I stood on the tee of the final hole. Surely nothing, nothing at all, could happen on one hole that would let Sharkey catch me.

I opened up with my big swing. Visions of the District flashed through my head. Good drive. Good three wood. Now an eight iron to the green, all open in front of me—not a tree or a trap in the way. I reached in my golf bag and pulled out an eight iron, but the instant I saw it, I knew it wasn't my eight iron. Hadn't I shined up all my clubs last night? The face on this club was stained green. Something was wrong. Very wrong. I checked my clubs again and found my own eight iron. What were two eight irons doing in my bag?

I had no idea how long I stood frozen in the middle of the fairway, hanging on to two clubs.

"Get a move on," Sharkey said. "Cantcha see we're holding up the foursome behind us?"

"I have two eight irons," I said.

A cunning look passed over Sharkey's face. "What a shame," she said, but her voice sounded triumphant. "That gives you fifteen clubs, one more than the rules allow."

"So what does that mean?"

"A four-stroke penalty," Sharkey said.

I put the extra iron back in my bag and addressed the ball. But I began to shake. I almost missed the shot. Another bad shot and several putts later, I finished the hole with an eight plus a four-stroke penalty. An even dozen.

My luck had run out.

"Sign here." Sharkey thrust the score card at me.

"No!" I cried. "I won't sign. Not until I find out my rights. I'm talking to the Rules Committee. I didn't put that extra iron in my bag. Someone else did."

I glared at Sharkey.

She shrugged, and I felt my stomach tremble.

The chairman of the Rules Committee was hawk-nosed, sharp-chinned, with a peaked visor pulled down over her brow.

"What is your problem?" she asked.

"On the final hole," I told her, "I discovered an extra eight iron in my bag. I don't know who put it there, but I know it wasn't there when I started."

"How can you be so sure?" She pushed up her visor and looked at me.

I corrected myself. "At least it wasn't in my bag when I left home. I washed and polished all my clubs last night so I know exactly how many I had, and this"—I pulled out the offending club—"was not among them."

The chairman inspected it. "Same length as yours," she said, "but not part of your set." She turned to Sharkey. "What do you know about this?"

Sharkey said, "First I knew about that club was when she pulled it out of her bag. I never expected anything like that." Sharkey held up her bag. "See, I got all my own clubs and none other."

The chairman studied Sharkey's eight iron, then returned it to Sharkey's bag. "A matching set and all there," she pronounced.

"It hardly seems fair—" I began.

"The rules are clear," the chairman said. "Each player is responsible for his own clubs, and that number must not exceed fourteen. Fair or not, you will have to accept the penalty." She shook her head and frowned. "But I'm sorry about this. We will do our best to get to the bottom of the problem. As each girl finishes, I personally will check her clubs, and I'll see that the pro at each park checks the clubs of the girls who have already left for home. We'll be in touch with you, and with your pro at Willow Tree."

There was nothing more I could do. Unwillingly I signed the card and with dragging feet I returned to the parking lot. A spate of questions greeted me as I opened the door to the station wagon.

"How did it go?"

"What did you shoot?"

"Did you shellac Sharkey?"

I gave my score, adding, "With twelve on the last hole."

An audible gasp as Lora cried, "You could have won today if it hadn't been for that Dirty Dozen!"

I slid into the front seat alongside Danny. In a halting voice I explained about the extra eight iron and the four-stroke penalty because of it.

Lora snorted. "I told you to watch out for *her.*"

"I know, I know. I thought I was on top of everything, then this had to happen."

Danny backed out of the parking slot and eased the wagon onto the expressway, slow going, since the factories were out. "What makes you both so sure that Sharkey had something to do with that eight iron?" he asked.

"Because that's just the way her mind works," Lora said. She leaned forward, talking over Danny's shoulder. "Believe me, I don't think it's nice to accuse anyone without proof, but maybe now is the time a few little items ought to surface. The last time I played Sharkey in a tournament, I saw her ball roll over in the rough. She didn't call the penalty on herself, so I brought the matter up. She looked me dead in the eye and said, 'You're seeing things. I guess I know when my ball moves better'n you do.'" Lora's voice rose with indignation. "Now if that isn't cheating, then lying on top of cheating, what is?"

"Still, that isn't the same as deliberately planting a club in someone's bag," Danny said as he accelerated into an outside lane.

"Sharkey is quite capable of anything," Lora said, "and if her dirty tricks keep Kate out of the District—" She tapped my shoulder. "You never told us. Where did you finish in the field?"

"Sharkey was fourth, and I dropped to sixth."

"Great!" Lora's eyes brightened. "Last year six were admitted into the District from the city program. You're in, I just know you are."

"I wouldn't be so sure." A chilly finger ran up my hot spine. "I have the funniest feeling that I just blew something."

11

Shenfield," the bus driver announced in ringing tones. "All out for Shenfield."

Actually I was the only one getting off. I stepped from the smoky hot bus into the sweet, cool country air and started down a rutted lane. My weekend with Aunt Lucy had come just when I needed it. I had to get away, away from all the talk-talk-talk about the extra club someone had put in my bag.

"Enjoy," I told myself. I crossed over a drainage ditch and followed a pebbled drive up to a house perched on the edge of a ravine. I stood on the overhanging porch and looked down on a stream with cattails standing ramrod straight in the driving current. Along the bank, chains of marsh marigolds spattered bright touches among the green ferns. There was the song of birds and the flash of wings.

Suddenly the door flew open and Aunt Lucy folded me in her arms. "Don't want to rush you, sweetie," she said, drawing me inside and taking my suitcase. "What I really mean to say is that we do have to rush. The club just called and said Meg Winchester won her match and is standing by for an interview."

"Meg Winchester. I've been following her progress report in the paper. Last year's champ, right?"

"And the year before that. Now it's a certainty that she will be defending her title tomorrow." Aunt Lucy breezed along the hall, setting the suitcase down outside a bedroom door. "I want to get Meg's story today so I can write it up and have it ready to file the minute tomorrow's match is over."

"I have lots to learn," I said. "Imagine writing up a match that hasn't even been played!"

"Of course, there may be a few last-minute changes, but at least I'll have all the background material. Meg's favored, you understand, and it'd be a real upset if she didn't win."

Aunt Lucy made a leap for the stairs. "I must find my notebook. I jotted down some questions I want to ask her."

"Tell me where it is and I'll get it for you."

"Believe me, you'll never find it, and I only hope I do," Aunt Lucy said.

Trudging up the stairs behind a flying Aunt Lucy, I thought again what a crazy upside-down house this was. The bedrooms, dining room and kitchen were on the lower level. The dining room wasn't much, but the kitchen was carpeted, on the theory that if the kitchen didn't look like a kitchen Aunt Lucy wouldn't mind cooking, and as she put it, Uncle Robb had the revolting habit of eating three times a day. On the upper level, a glass-walled living room overlooked the ravine, and at the back, double dens marked HIS and HERS were windowless. "I don't want any distractions while I work."

The door to Uncle Robb's den was open. There was a gleaming leather-top desk with a clock and a barometer, bookshelves, a red leather chair.

"There's only one rule around here," Aunt Lucy laughed merrily. "I don't go into Uncle

Robb's office without an invitation and he doesn't come into mine without one. Since he said he wouldn't be caught dead in my sanctuary, this has never been a serious problem." She flung open the door to her den and I took an involuntary step backward.

"Don't look so shocked, sweetie. It may look a tad tacky, but everything's orderly enough once you understand the filing system. Those papers on my desk, material for my column. The papers on the studio couch, the Great American Novel that I've been working on since college. The papers on the corner table, an article for *Better Homes and Gardens,* once I do the rewrite. And over there—"

"But, Aunt Lucy, why would you ever paper the wall above your typewriter with rejection slips? I should think all those 'We regret to inform you's' would get you down when you're working on something new."

"I call that my Wailing Wall, or, if you prefer, my keep-me-humble wall. Every time I get my hopes up that I've written something that will rock the world, I look up from my typewriter and I say, 'Cool it!'"

I leaned against the door frame and gave an understanding nod. "You don't get rejection slips playing golf, but a score card can tear you to bits and pieces." I proceeded to run off a rapid-fire account of the city championship.

"I'm so proud of you," Aunt Lucy said. "A first-year golfer up there with the best."

Aunt Lucy didn't seem to understand. I tried again. "But if it hadn't been for that extra eight iron—and even Bix can't figure out how it got in my bag unless, of course, someone just happened to plant it there so she'd win and I'd lose—"

"Now, sweetie," Aunt Lucy said as she banged shut another desk drawer, "I'm terribly sorry about the penalty for your sake. What an unhappy end to a great game! But accidents do happen. I'll never forget watching the Bermuda Classic on TV with the big winner carrying an extra club in his bag, and surely you'd think with all that money riding on his game, he'd know better than to tee off with two putters."

I didn't answer that. I didn't want Aunt Lucy to think I was a poor sport. Anyway, why drag Sharkey into the picture when Aunt Lucy had never heard of her?

"At last," Aunt Lucy said, producing a notebook from under a manuscript. "And no one but myself to blame for losing it!"

Ten minutes later Aunt Lucy charged her red compact out of the drive, banking the curves along the road that led to Swan Lake Country Club as if she were trying to cut a fraction of a second in the Indy 500. She rounded a corner and skidded between the fieldstone posts that marked the entrance to the club. Waving a press pass at a startled guard, she gunned the car up the hill.

With a flick of the wheel, she pinched the compact into a corner space. Above us, the white clapboard clubhouse stretched along a knoll, long and low with white pillars supporting the roof over a front veranda. Flowers everywhere—lemon lilies, larkspur, snapdragons in a medley of color.

"It's beautiful," I told Aunt Lucy, "but where does the Swan Lake come in?"

"You can't see the lake from here. But beyond the eighteenth green there's a lovely little lake with a family of swans. The swans have become pets, except in mating season, when they attack anyone unfortunate enough to hook a ball in their direction."

"Sand hazards and water hazards and now swan hazards." I laughed.

"Ah, but it's not always a laughing matter. More than once an angry swan has determined the outcome of a close match." She shrugged. "But I doubt very much if someone as straight and accurate as Meg Winchester is even aware that there are swans around here."

Behind the rope barricade, tall and short girls, not unlike the girls I saw day after day at Willow Tree Park, were hitting shag balls out on the practice range. Such distance! And such accuracy, I decided, as I watched the girls chip to the practice green. My eyes grooved in on a willowy blond who dropped wedge after wedge into the exact center of the green.

"I'll have to revise my thinking," I said. "If I land a wedge on the green, I think I've got it made. That blond acts as if she expects each and every ball to sink from twenty yards out."

"You have a good eye for experts," Aunt Lucy said. "That's Meg Winchester."

"Wow!"

Meg finished her bucket of balls and, turning, noticed Aunt Lucy. She stepped over the rope—not too difficult a feat with her long legs—and walked toward us. Close up this way, I could see the blue eyes and fair skin underneath the broad-brimmed golf hat. She had broad shoulders and narrow hips and wore her golf outfit with a touch of class. Altogether a knockout.

"Congratulations on your victory today." Aunt Lucy smiled.

"Thank you." Meg spoke in a bored voice, as if talking to reporters and giving interviews was a bit of a nuisance but something expected of her.

"What was the final outcome?"

Meg told her and Aunt Lucy perked up.

"A big win," Aunt Lucy said.

"Bigger than last year."

"And tomorrow your victim will be?" Aunt Lucy poised her pencil above her notebook.

Meg gestured toward the golf course. "Amy Mandel and Chipper Daley are still out there playing. At last report, Amy was ahead."

"I'm surprised you're not watching."

"I'd rather not."

"What do you plan to do after you win tomorrow?"

Meg smiled a little, showing her perfect teeth. "I'm going to treat myself to a couple of days of rest. I've played one hundred holes of competitive golf so far this week, with the finals still to come."

"Such stamina!" Aunt Lucy said. "And I know every player who has come here is out to beat you."

"So they tell me."

"How does that affect your strategy?"

"I get off to a charging start, and then hang on to my lead." Meg gave a little shrug. "I find the competition wilts after a bit."

"As I understand it," Aunt Lucy said, "the winner and the runner-up of this tournament are invited to play in the Women's National Amateur."

"I plan to be there," Meg said.

Aunt Lucy wrote furiously. "And if you do as well in that as you've done in this, it is likely that you'll be asked to represent America on the Curtis Cup team in England, and later play on the Women's World Amateur team in Australia."

Meg smiled mysteriously, and I held my breath. Imagine—golf around the world!

A roar reverberated from someplace out on the golf course. Meg cocked her head. "The match must be over."

Crowds surged over the hills. The pro dashed up to Meg.

"You will play Chipper Daley in the finals tomorrow. Tee off at nine thirty."

"Chipper?" A brow lifted in surprise.

"You've played Chipper before," Aunt Lucy said.

"Several times."

"And you've always won?"

"Yes." Meg rubbed her hands together in a there's-nothing-to-it gesture.

Aunt Lucy closed her notebook and we walked back toward the car.

"Meg acts as if the whole thing is already over," I said. "Did you notice how she's made plans for doing this and that after she wins the tournament?"

"Confidence is a great thing," Aunt Lucy said. "Especially if it's backed up with know-how."

"If you ask me, she seems too sure."

Aunt Lucy smiled, and I knew that she'd made up her mind to feature Meg as a three-time winner.

12

I'm all hyped up!" I raced ahead of Aunt Lucy, then stopped and waited. "I couldn't be more excited, unless I were playing myself."

"Maybe next year you will be." Aunt Lucy adjusted her sunglasses and looked at me through oversized lenses.

"Ha. Meg Winchester would make mince-meat of me."

"I didn't say you'd make the finals. Maybe you wouldn't even qualify. But if you get your handicap low enough, it would be a wonderful experience."

"Experience! That's the line Bix keeps

feeding me." My mind soared on an intoxicating flight of fantasy.

The first tee at Swan Lake was a far cry from the utilitarian mound of earth at Willow Tree Park. It curved into the hillside almost as if it were a stage setting for the players. There was a platform of green grass and a stone wall backdrop blooming with purple, pink, and white clematis. Below, the fairway stretched almost five hundred yards to the green. A red flag, barely visible from where I was standing, hung limp on the flagstick.

No one was playing—no one at all. The whole course, five miles of it, was ready and waiting for two girls, girls not much older than I. One would win. One would lose. What were they thinking? Feeling?

"I only hope it won't rain today," Aunt Lucy said, a remark so far from my thoughts it brought me up short.

"Whatever made you think of rain on a day like this?" I asked, scanning the blue, sunny sky.

"Well, Wednesday started out without a cloud. By noon it was raining hard, then harder. The players were drowned rats when they got back to the locker room. It would be bad luck if the finals had to be played in the rain."

"I've only played in the rain once," I said, "and you can have it. I quit after a couple of holes. If you ask me, it's not right to make anyone play in the rain."

"Hardly a question of right or wrong," Aunt Lucy said. "Tournaments are set up too far in advance to be changed at the last minute because of the weather. Besides, rain is part of the golf scene, like high winds or a bad lie. Good players learn to cope. Naturally, if there's lightning, the tournament is called off."

"Bix warned us. He said there's no better conductor of lightning than steel-shafted clubs and cleats in golf shoes and to run, not walk, to the nearest shelter."

"Shelter, yes, but trees, no." Aunt Lucy swung around. "Here *she* comes, with Meg and Chipper, and just look at the crowd, would you?" Aunt Lucy scribbled a flurry of letters in the black notebook. A.C. USGAJC OT

"But, Aunt Lucy, you'll never be able to translate that."

"Sweetie, it goes like this: A.C.—Mrs. Axford Collingwood—and the next letters tell me that she is a representative of the United States Golf Association's Junior Committee."

"But what's OT?"

"That you should guess. On time. It's exactly nine thirty."

Mrs. Collingwood spoke into a hand mike. "On the tee, Meg Winchester, Cypress Point, Pebble Beach, California, defending champion."

Meg looked upbeat in all pink—the skirt, the shell, the hat with the narrow brim—even pink pom-poms on the white socks. Her fair skin was pinkish too and glistening with oil.

"Doesn't she look smashing?" The lady behind me cooed.

"She plays smashing too," the friend assented.

Meg teed up her ball and the crowd pressed against the ropes. With the assurance of a born winner, she stepped right up and, without so much as a practice swing, sent the ball whistling two hundred yards down the fairway.

The crowd cheered. Meg had the gallery going for her.

"On the tee," Mrs. Collingwood intoned, and it may have been my imagination, but there seemed to be a funereal note in the announcement. "Chipper Daley, Sand Valley, North Carolina."

Chipper was thin and wiry, with cropped black hair, a pug nose overshadowed by a square jaw. She took a wide stance, wound up, and arched her back into a bow.

"Good heavens!" Aunt Lucy said. "She's made of elastic."

A fast swing, powering through the ball with every ounce of clout in her scrawny frame. The ball streaked forward, then veered off into the rough. No applause, only mutterings.

"Bad drive," Aunt Lucy said.

"Bad break, you mean."

Bad! It was a great effort, only a little off line. I sent out good vibes to this girl I'd never seen before. Why did I feel this way? Was it because Chipper was the underdog, or was it because I played the same kind of game—the big swing that meant the bigger margin of error?

Chipper moved fast. She picked up her bag—a bag that looked as if it had been around since the beginning of time—and I wasn't at all sure Chipper had the full complement of clubs she was allowed to carry. She sprinted down the rough. I knew what she was thinking. It would be awfully easy to lose a ball in that tangle of deep grass.

The crowd gathered around Meg. "The Winchester Worshipers" Aunt Lucy called them.

"Well, I'm betting on Chipper," I said, a stubborn jut to my jaw.

"But, sweetie, she doesn't have much of a chance." Aunt Lucy added. "But even if she loses, she's done a super job getting as far as the finals. She hails from a little town in North Carolina with a single city-run golf course, and that in bad shape. She takes a bus over to Pinehurst once a season and works with an old pro, but for the most part she's self-taught. She came all the way here in a cartage truck just so she could play."

I worried right along with Chipper about the ball buried in the matted grass, what Lora called "unfriendly rough." But Chipper got out—something I could never have done—and made a super shot to the green. It did her no good. Meg rammed in a long putt and the hole was lost.

At the end of three holes, Chipper was three down.

"Not a match," the lady behind me said to her friend, "but a slaughter."

I wanted to shout, "You're all wrong! Just wait and see!" But they had already started back toward the clubhouse.

For Meg things were going according to her game plan. Steamroll the opposition at the start, then watch the opposition wilt.

Only Chipper wasn't wilting. I cheered as she

kept coming on stronger and stronger, but no matter what she did, she never made up the three holes she'd lost at the beginning of the match.

On the sixteenth tee Aunt Lucy put her notebook into her tote bag.

"It's not over yet," I said. I planted my feet firmly, my toes curling.

"A great match, sweetie, but there's no way. From now on a tie isn't good enough. Chipper would have to win all three and that would be asking for miracles."

"Well, what's the matter with a miracle?"

Aunt Lucy smiled indulgently.

At that moment Chipper's shot took a sideways kick and settled back of a small tree, stymied.

"That's the worst break I've ever seen, and at a crucial time like this!"

I waited for Chipper to tap the ball out from behind the tree, as Lora and I would have done. But Chipper had something else in mind. She walked forward to study the position of the flagstick on the green.

Aunt Lucy checked her watch. "Really," she said, "with that tree in her way, why worry about the pin? I wish she'd get on with it, so I could file my story."

At last Chipper took her stance, a hook stance, and sent the ball flying. It skinned the trunk of the tree heading for the trap and then, like a boomerang, it changed course, hooking in toward the green and dropping within two feet of the flagstick.

"How about that?" I shouted triumphantly, thrilled as if I myself had made the miracle shot.

"Well, I must admit the kid's unflappable." Aunt Lucy rescued her notebook from her tote bag.

The crowd applauded wildly. They favored Meg, but still they appreciated a stunning golf shot.

Obviously flustered, Meg lost the hole. And who could blame her? It isn't often that someone stymied by a tree, really out of contention, suddenly is back in the game.

The impossible happened again on the next hole. Chipper made a masterful explosion out of a trap for a "gimme" putt. And when on the eighteenth a swan took out after Meg, Meg picked up her ball and conceded.

"It wasn't even a mating swan." Aunt Lucy shook her head in confusion. "All Meg had to do was finish in regulation for a win."

Now a "sudden death" playoff. Champion that she was, Meg pulled herself together. Too late. Chipper, who overshot the green, chipped the ball back into the cup.

"Now you know why she's nicknamed Chipper." Aunt Lucy wrote rapidly as she talked. "She may not be the greatest putter, but there's scarcely a round when she doesn't chip a ball in."

Meg shook hands with Chipper and the two girls walked in side by side, fans following. As they reached the clubhouse, a truck with TV cameras moved into position and a sportscaster appeared on the scene.

"Today," he said in a jaunty voice that went along with his checked shirt and gaudy tie, "has been one of the most sensational matches in the annals of Junior Golf. There has been an upset." He turned to Chipper. "I hope you don't mind if I refer to you as a dark horse?"

Chipper grinned. "Call me a donkey if you like."

The sportscaster turned to Meg. Her pink cheeks had paled. She looked tired. "You are defending champion," he said. "You were leading all the way. How do you account for the final outcome?"

"I took too much for granted." Meg held her beautiful head high and I thought what a great sport she was in this moment of defeat. "Three down and three to go. It never occurred to me that anyone could come back from that position."

"And how do you account for that saving sand shot?" The sportscaster addressed Chipper.

"Where I come from, Sand Valley, North Carolina, there's nothing *but* sand."

"There you are, sports fans. Two lovely American girls—a champion who blames her defeat on overconfidence and a comer from North Carolina who can pull rabbits out of hats, or, more specifically, perfect wedges out of traps."

The cameras swung around, beaming in on the president of the United States Golf Association, who had flown in from New York to present the awards.

"It is my pleasure to present the Glenna Collectt Vare Trophy to the winner of the United States Girls' Junior Championship. As you know, Glenna Collectt was our country's most outstanding golfer."

On with it, I thought as the president enumerated Collectt's fifty-nine victories in major competition. My ears pricked up when I heard Chipper's name.

"Today, Chipper Daley, you join the ranks of

America's great junior golfers. Your name will be engraved on this trophy for posterity, and you will be given a replica of this cup as a lifetime memorial of this event."

Chipper stepped forward, her face as bright and shining as the silver trophy she held in her arms. I wondered if the impossible might ever happen to me, if sometime *my* name would be engraved on this historic cup.

"For you, Meg Winchester," the president said, "as runner-up of this tournament, it is my pleasure to present you with a Silver Pin."

Meg accepted graciously, but I could see the deep disappointment behind the plastic smile. The pin seemed so little compared to the glory of winning the cup.

"Hurry, Kate," Aunt Lucy prodded me after the Bronze Pins had been awarded, "or we'll never make the awards dinner on time." She dashed down the hall in the clubhouse. "I have to get to a phone. All kinds of changes to make in my column."

"I told you Chipper would come through," I said, thinking to myself, Who ever would have believed it?

13

Shafts of late-day sun poured through the casement windows, scoring the carpet with geometric patterns of gold. The carpet was deep green, the walls a lighter green, and the ceiling the palest tint of all.

I hesitated on the threshold. In that room, nothing but strangers.

Aunt Lucy made a sweeping wall-to-wall gesture. "When the room's empty, all that green is a bit much, but with all you gorgeous gals making a splash, it has to be the prettiest place in the club."

I nodded, too nervous to speak.

"You look terrific." Aunt Lucy gave my hand a quick squeeze. "All that golf has made you elegantly slim, like a model."

"No put-ons, please," I said stiffly. But Aunt Lucy had made her point. I stood up taller, straighter, playacting the model role.

Aunt Lucy pinned a hostess tag on me and a press tag on herself.

"Me? A hostess?"

"You didn't play in the tournament, you're not an official, so you have to be a hostess."

"What does that mean?" Alarm bells rang in my head.

Aunt Lucy's eyes darted around the room. "Everyone's so busy gabbing, no one's even noticed the canapés in the far corner. So if you don't mind passing—"

My mouth watered. I heaped one plate with hot things—french-fried shrimps, mini meatballs, and baby franks—and another plate with olives, radishes and carrot curls. I moved from group to group. Now and then I caught snatches of conversation.

"This has been my mostest vacation," a redhead exulted as she stabbed a shrimp on a pick and dipped it in seafood sauce. "I've never seen such a heavenly course or such hellish traps. At home we just roll the ball out. But here there's oceans of sand and an overhanging lip and I just couldn't cope."

"I built my own trap for practice," I found myself saying. The redhead turned to me, eyes questioning. I told her about the pit I'd dug in the Dubois' yard and all about the obstacle course at Lora's.

"Am I ever glad I ran into you!" the girl enthused. "I don't know why I never thought of that myself, but as soon as I get back to Kansas I'm going to start digging."

Everyone laughed.

"I mean it," the girl said. "Wait until I come up against you next year—you won't have a chance."

I edged through a circle of chairs, feeling more than a little pleased that I'd been able to make a suggestion that might benefit a tournament player.

Someone in blue waved. "Don't go away. I'm starving."

I held out the hot plate. A tanned hand speared three meatballs on one pick.

"If you're such a pig," the plump kid alongside her said, "how come you're so thin?"

"It's like this. When I'm playing a match and the heat's on, I can hardly eat at all. I was really embarrassed this morning. I'm staying in this lady's house and she got up early and cooked ham and waffles for me. 'Eat hearty,' she said, 'and you'll play better.' But I couldn't swallow. Now that the match is over—"

I blinked and looked at the girl in blue more closely. Chipper Daley! She had appeared one way on the course—wiry, tense, determined— but now she was relaxed, her short hair curling over her ears, ruffles soft around her throat, a locket dangling on a linked chain.

"Hi! I'm Kate Morrison. I was pulling for you all the way," I said.

"I'm glad to hear that!" Chipper giggled. "The Gallup Poll would have counted me out. I was not the people's choice."

I glanced uncertainly around the room.

Chipper must have read me. "Meg's not here. She left right after the awards. But you can count on one thing: She'll be back, winning again."

"So will you," I said. "I never saw anything like it, clinching the match with a chip in! Someone called it nothing but luck, but I won-der—"

"It's exactly like an old pro in Pinehurst says—the better you chip, the more luck you have."

The plump girl gulped an olive. "Boy, am I ever schizo! If I'm losing, I know right then and there that the situation is going to deteriorate and it always does."

An expectant hush as Chipper fingered the little gold locket. "My secret weapon," she said. She unsnapped it and passed it around the circle. Engraved inside the heart-shaped case were three words—NEVER GIVE UP.

I felt a thump in my head, a gavel pounding some sense into me. Chipper had been in impossible shape today, but she had succeeded. Why had I given up so easily? Why had I let the penalty on the last hole at Metro cause my downfall? I could still have won if I hadn't let up.

"Come along, sweetie." Aunt Lucy took me by the elbow. "I want you to meet a friend of mine—Mrs. Golf."

I set the canapés on a side table and followed Aunt Lucy. I knew all about Mrs. Golf. So much depended on her. She worked along with the pros at the public courses and helped decide which girls would be chosen for the District.

Wise old eyes set in a weathered, deeply wrinkled face peered at me.

"I've seen you someplace!" She wagged a knarled finger. "Sometimes I forget a name, but seldom a face, and never a swing."

"I play at Willow Tree Park," I said.

"Of course, of course! You're the girl with the big swing. I saw you come up to the eighteenth green—shoot over it, actually."

"I didn't see you," I said.

"Ah! You weren't supposed to. But I was impressed."

My cheeks flushed.

Mrs. Golf rushed on. "I've been so busy with this national affair, I've neglected my local girls. But I intend to catch up. How did you do at Metro?"

"Best I've ever done. Then—" I told Mrs. Golf about the extra club in my bag and my final score.

"How frightful! At times like that it's hard to believe that the rules are there for your own protection." She sighed. "Only sorry there isn't room in the District for all you promising young players!"

Was Mrs. Golf making conversation or was she trying to tell me that I'd blown my chance? The palms of my hands began to prickle with a thousand invisible needles.

The sensation passed when Chipper said,

"There's an extra place at our table, Kate. How about it?"

"You'll have to talk fast!" Lora said breathlessly when I reached her on the phone.

"Why so?"

"Father put in a new rule. Only three minutes a call. When we pick up the receiver, we turn a little hourglass over. Wow—the sand's running through like crazy. Say something!"

"Forget it. I couldn't begin to tell you what it's like in the big league with stars like Meg Winchester and Chipper Daley and all the exciting things that happened while some itsy-bitsy sand runs through."

"I want to hear! Honest I do!" Lora's cry of distress rang in my ears. "Soon's I get through a mountain of dishes, I can escape. How about meeting me at the park in an hour?"

"Sure." I cleared my throat. "Any news about the eight iron?"

"Bix is still working on it, but nothing yet. I hear that even *he* is beginning to suspect *her*."

"Who else?"

"I understand that Bix is setting up a special match between the two of you, a once-and-for-all playoff."

"I'd like that," I said tersely. "When?"

"Don't know the details." Lora broke off. "Going, going, gone—the sand, I mean. Bye for now."

My mind was revved up. I went out to the garage and got on my bike. So Bix was not accepting the outcome of the city championship. I was going to get another chance. And now that Chipper had shared her secret for success—*Never give up*—I was going to hang in there all the way.

I coasted down the drive and out into the street. A screech of tires! A car swerved. I swerved. My heart began to pound. A close call.

Mr. Dubois jumped out of the front seat. "Are you all right, Kate?"

"Yes. Thanks to you," I added shakily. "I don't know what's with me. My mind was a million miles away." I glimpsed a figure huddled in the front seat of the Dubois car. "Say, isn't that Mrs. Dubois?"

"Home from the hospital. Isn't that the best news?"

"You bet. Let me help."

"I can manage," Mr. Dubois said, but quickly changed his mind. "Two is better than one. All that bed rest makes a body weak."

Mr. Dubois opened the car door and I tried not to register shock. The change in Mrs. Dubois was alarming. Her skin had taken on a yellowish tinge and was drawn tightly over her high cheekbones. But when she spoke it was as if everything was quite the same.

"Good to see you, Kate."

"Welcome home," I said.

"I'm not one to be cooped up." She swung her feet around into the open door. "I've missed the sky, the trees, the grass." She turned toward Mr. Dubois. "I'd like to sit outdoors a spell."

We helped her stand. Her bony fingers dug into my forearm.

"Hope I'm not leaning too heavily."

"That's my golf arm, good and strong."

Slowly we made our way across the yard. Every bird on the block gathered to sing joyful hosannas in celebration of the homecoming. Mrs. Dubois paused by the vegetable garden, catching her breath.

"The tomatoes are almost ripe," she said. "Won't be long before I can get at the canning."

She's too sick to can, I thought. Too sick for anything. Still, she was talking as if this August were like all the other Augusts. How old was she? Much older than Mom and Dad, but too young to—

Tenderly Mr. Dubois lowered the thin body down into the wicker chair under the apple tree. Leaf shadows made dancing patterns at her feet. She let out a wispy sigh, then slowly seemed to recover a modicum of strength. Rheumy eyes roamed the garden as if looking for something, then came to rest on the sundial. *Count none but sunny hours.* Slack lips curved into a smile and her hand reached out for Mr. Dubois, and he took her hand in his.

"Your beautiful," he said. His eyes glistened.

Silently I backed away. There was Mrs. Dubois, old, sick, ugly, and he called her beautiful, and I knew that was exactly the way he saw her.

I pedaled hard and fast. A barking dog alerted me to a car banking around the corner. Ron. My heart gave an unwanted lurch. I pedaled on, eyes straight ahead. There was the sound of grinding wheels as the car went into reverse.

"Hey, Kate!" Ron leaned out the window, his hair blowing rakishly back from his forehead. "If you'd travel on foot, I'd give you a lift."

"I'll remember that."

"Can you spare a moment?" he said.

"Just."

"Well, then, come sit in the car with me."

I didn't like the way he took it for granted that I'd jump at his bidding. Still, I was curious.

"This is a break for me," Ron said, and pushed open the car door, "running into you like this. I can never get you alone. Mimi's always around, and if I phone, well, she's the one who answers."

"That figures."

"Mimi tells me there's someone who goes along with the golf package. And who is this Danny?"

I shrugged.

"Oh, c'mon."

"A golfing friend, that's all."

Ron leaned toward me and gently stoked my hair back over my ears and his dark eyes held mine.

"Kate, forgive?"

"For what?" I tried to keep it cool—not easy when every part of me was on fire. Even my earlobes were hot where he'd touched them.

"Okay, okay. The scenario reads like this. Boy and girl are a team. Boy meets Golden Girl and the team splits. Boy learns that all that glitters is not gold. In fact, he learns he's made one helluva mistake, and he says, Please, Kate, let's be partners again."

Eyes shut against the sun, shut against all outside distractions, I listened to the voice that had a hypnotic effect on me. Ron had spoken the words that in my secret dreams I most wanted to hear. If only I could believe him! Maybe time would prove I could. But the scenario didn't quite ring true. Only last week Golden Girl had discovered Lifeguard, and she was getting curiouser and curiouser about Danny.

And, of course, September was coming up fast. The partnership would give me the privilege of spending hours in the library doing the research and hours at my desk doing the writing for his debating speeches.

"I'll have to think about it," I said, and opened the car door.

Ron put his hand on my knee. "Now, Kate, don't play hard to get."

If only he knew how easy I was to get! But first things first. I still had Sharkey to beat.

Besides, it wouldn't hurt Ron to wait. Even though he was as handsome and dashing as ever, there was something about him I decided that wasn't quite genuine or real. Something I didn't like. Was he a little too conceited for my taste? Quite suddenly I decided I preferred shy people—or at least people who didn't always appear to think about themselves first, like Mimi—and yes, like Ron.

14

Bix speaking." The voice was urgent. "Can you get here right away?"

"I'm barely awake and there's a leak in my bike tire and—"

"Danny will come for you. You'll be playing Sharkey in half an hour."

"Play Sharkey? Now? Today?" I pressed the receiver closer to my ear, waiting for an explanation, but there was only a click as Bix hung up.

I hated all this rush-rush before a match, but what could I do? Danny was at the door before I'd even finished my cereal.

"If I'd known I had to play Sharkey today"—

I trotted down the walk side by side with Danny—"I never would have stayed up for 'The Late Late Show.'"

Danny swung the car around and headed for the park. "Bix is leaving today."

"Oh, no!" I gapsed.

"Oh, yes." Danny's big hands locked around the wheel, as if he needed something to hang on to. He glanced at me out of the corner of his eye. "It hit me hard too."

"But, Danny, isn't this awful sudden?"

"Well, we all knew he was going to pull out just as soon as Doc said the knee was okay. The X rays came through. The knee is as good as new—anyway, good enough for the circuit. Bix starts driving tonight. That way he'll make the Open in time."

I leaned back, trying to sort things out in my mind. "If Bix is so pressed for time," I said, "why bother with us? Sharkey and I could play off later."

"It does seem crazy," Danny agreed. "But he refers to your match as unfinished business."

"That's big of him, to care about what happens to us." I spoke up bravely. "I'm really happy for him."

"You don't sound it," Danny said.

"I am. I want Battling Bix to battle his way to

the top. Only"—I couldn't help the tremor in my voice—"without him, nothing will ever be the same for me."

Danny nodded as if he understood. He stopped in front of the clubhouse, idling the motor.

"I don't suppose there's any news about the eight iron," I asked for the hundredth time.

Danny shook his head. "And when Bix goes, there's that much less chance of finding where it came from."

"I never did think anyone would claim it." I stepped out of the car, shouldering my bag. "But I'm going to forget the whole bit before it jinxes my game."

"Play well," Danny called after me. "We'll celebrate later."

"Howdy," Sharkey said as I approached the first tee. She was pumping the handle of the ball washer, sloshing soapy water onto the grass. "Can I wash your balls for you?"

"No thanks," I said. My fingertips tingled, a sort of electronic warning that Sharkey had something other than washing balls in mind. With utmost care, I counted my clubs to be sure each one was there, and no spares.

Bix sprinted toward us, with a far livelier gait than earlier in the summer.

My eyes met his. "I'll miss you," I said.

"Appreciate the thought, but on with the match, and as soon as it's over, pick up your balls and report back to me." He placed the score card in my hand, and his smile flashed a message of encouragement. I felt he wanted me to win, and win for him I must—a parting gift for all he'd done for me.

"I'm ready," I said.

Ready for golf. Ready for Sharkey. With confidence I stepped up onto the tee and opened up with my big swing. A crack like a bullet. A *whoosh* of air. The ball rocketed off the club head, soaring into space.

"You'll never hit a bigger one," Bix said.

Sharkey slammed the ball a long distance too, but it tailed into the rough. It was good to be on the fairway. I was sick and tired of always being the girl in the rough.

"Too bad," I said politely as I saw her bum lie. And when Sharkey's second shot buried in a trap, I felt that rotten luck was just what she deserved. The first hole was an easy win, and taking my cue from Meg Winchester, I started to solidify my lead, making it difficult, if not impossible, for Sharkey to catch up.

It wasn't until the seventh hole that I became aware of the changing light. The overcast sky darkened and on the horizon cumulous clouds piled up into thunderheads.

"Hope it won't rain," I said.

"Oh, it's going to rain all right." Sharkey's small eyes squinted at the sky. "But if the match goes fast, we'll get in first. A little rain never hurt no one."

The rain held off until the second nine. It wasn't much of a rain—just a steady drizzle. Sharkey got out her golf umbrella and it protected her and her clubs.

"Better put up your umbrella," she said.

"I don't have one," I said.

Of course I could have borrowed Mom's—a small umbrella was better than none—but I'd left in such a hurry I'd never even thought of rain. Aunt Lucy had said rain was part of the game, but not the part I like, I decided now as my damp shirt clung to my ribs.

The rain beat down harder and Sharkey said, "Come under the umbrella with me. There's plenty of room for the both of us."

Feeling that I'd rather drown than share anything with Sharkey, I declined and walked ahead. But the rain was ruining me. I addressed the ball with my three wood, the club I could always count on. But I couldn't find the sweet spot. The club was coated with soggy mud and the ball skidded only a few feet along the ground.

Disgusted, I shoved the wood back into the bag and brought out an iron. The grip slipped in my wet glove. Frantic, I rummaged around in the pocket of my bag for a towel. The towel helped until it became soaked, then it was swing and miss all over again. I eyed Sharkey's towel tucked up in the ribs of her umbrella, fluffy and dry. I was tempted to ask her if I could borrow it to wipe off my hands before each shot, then I quickly decided against asking anything of her. Why give her the opportunity to taunt me with a snide refusal. "So your clubs slip! Tough!"

Hole by hole my lead dwindled. The rain turned into a downpour. Instead of breathing, I seemed to be gulping water. It took all of my strength and all of my willpower to go on at all.

The match evened out and I tried to bolster my sagging spirits. *Never give up.* Still, there didn't seem to be much I could do to help myself. Sharkey, secure and dry, was playing as well as ever, but for me the simplest shot was a challenge and a problem.

Thunder growled in the distance. Sharkey hurried over to her ball and belted it down the final fairway.

"Make it snappy," she said, "so we can get the match over with. All hell is about to break loose."

I pushed forward against the rising wind. But as I reached my ball, lightning slashed the clouds like a fiery knife. An instantaneous crack of thunder banged my ears. The sky became a blinding sheet of light.

"Geez!" Sharkey cried. "Drop your clubs, Kate! Run for it!"

The sky suddenly was as black as it had been bright. My eyes tried to cut through the curtain of rain, but I could see no shelter. A twisting gust of wind whipped me around and I dove under a tree. The overhanging branches shielded me from the full force of rain and the trunk warded off the eye of the storm.

Lightning struck again—so close I smelled the ozone in the air. Another flash, and in that moment of brightness I saw Sharkey running toward me. A *clap-clap-clap* of thunder, and in that instant before the thunder cracked again, Sharkey's high, hysterical voice penetrated my senses.

"Kate, Kate, get out from under that tree!"

I leaped forward, just as a finger of lightning

pointed downward. An explosion of splintering wood. I tried to run, but my knees buckled.

Wheels sloshed through wet heavy grass and I looked up. Bix was standing over me. Strong arms helped me into the seat of a golf cart.

"Hurt?" he asked.

I stretched my arms and legs and neck and everything worked.

"Nothing a hot shower won't cure."

With Bix at my side and the storm abating, I felt calm, almost cheerful. The fright and shock I had just experienced had an unreal quality— like a nightmare that vanishes with the coming of day.

Bix gunned the pedal and headed back toward the clubhouse. His eyes snapped. "You know better than to stand under a tree in a storm. You've been warned about lightning again and again."

"It all happened so fast," I said. "If it hadn't been for a bloodcurdling scream at the right moment—" I shivered.

"Lucky for you," Bix said. He shook his head. "Close. Much too close."

"Let's say I wouldn't want to go through it again." I hugged my arms around my rib cage. "There were all kinds of vibrations and tremors, and I still don't know whether I tripped or whether I was knocked down, but everything went blank and black." I unfolded my arms and pushed strands of dripping hair out of my eyes. "It was Sharkey who screamed and I bet it was Sharkey who sent you out after me."

Bix gave a curt nod.

Inside the clubhouse I found Sharkey, but when I began to thank her, Bix took my arm and ushered me into his back office and closed the door.

"That will have to wait until later, Kate. I must talk to you, now, alone." He went around to the other side of the desk and gestured toward a chair. "Sit down," he said.

"Better that I stand and drip." I took the towel Bix handed me and rubbed my goose-fleshed arms and legs.

Bix twisted in his swivel chair. "There's a matter I must get settled before I leave. Mrs. Golf called and told me that no more than two girls will be admitted into the District from Willow Tree Park. Lora has number one place. It's you or Sharkey for second."

I held my breath.

"Here's the handicap book." Bix riffled through the pages. "Sharkey has a lower handicap, but that can be explained by the fact that you are a new player and naturally started off the season with higher scores. Sharkey beat you at Metro, but the penalty strokes on the final hole kept you from beating her. I had hoped today's playoff would be decisive, but all we found out was that you play superior golf if circumstances are favorable, and Sharkey comes through when experience counts."

"So," I said, my mouth suddenly dry, "what is your decision?"

Bix looked me squarely in the eye. "I want you to answer my questions honestly. There have been complaints about Sharkey, even rather serious accusations from Lora. I decided to have it out with Sharkey. She admits to a bit of gamesmanship, which I told her in no uncertain terms to cut out. But she swears she's never cheated. She said Lora was seeing things wrong because Lora didn't like her and saw only what she wanted to see. I told her she was on probation as far as I was concerned, and if there was one more report on her, no matter how trivial, I would never under any circumstances recommend her for the District. Tell me, how did she act today? Did she do anything that might be construed in a bad light?"

I braced myself against the desk. "As a matter of fact, she offered to wash my balls, and when the rain started she invited me to share her umbrella." I laughed mirthlessly. "If I'd known she was on her best behavior, I might have taken her up on that, and, well, things might have been very different."

"I'm sure good manners don't come easily to her, but I'm glad to hear she's trying." Bix stood up and paced the room. "There's still the question of the eight iron. I personally checked the clubs of each girl who played Metro that day. No dice. Now how do you suppose that club ever got in your bag?"

I said nothing.

"Did it ever cross your mind that Sharkey might have planted it there?"

"You asked me to be honest so I have to say yes to that one."

Bix said, "Were you ever aware of Sharkey fooling around with your clubs or your bag?"

I felt a sudden rush of blood to my head. Everything would depend on my answer. I was Bix's protégé. He wanted to recommend me for the District. More than anything I wanted to be in the District, drive with Lora next summer to all those super challenging courses in and around the city. The opportunity was mine, now. All I had to do was cast the tiniest bit of doubt on Sharkey, and I was so sure—

"When I stepped up on the first tee . . ." I began, averting my eyes to the window. Rain still sluiced down the panes, but the thunder was a distant rumble. The storm was moving on. Soon Bix would be moving on. "Out of the corner of my eye," I said, "I could see Sharkey—" *Go ahead and say it.* Tell Bix Sharkey was messing around with your clubs. He'll believe you. But the words I wanted to say stuck in my throat. "I didn't see a thing," I whispered hoarsely.

Bix exhaled slowly. "Then I will have to rely on the handicaps, and Sharkey will be recommended for the District." He put out his hand. "I appreciate your honesty."

"Thanks a bunch!" I turned and ran from the room. A noose tightened around my throat. Tears pressed against my eyelids. I started for the exit, but Sharkey grabbed me by the wrists.

"I knew it! I knew it!" I reeled forward, but Sharkey hung on. "Soon's Bix shut that office door, I knew you two was in cahoots. Now what story did you concoct to keep me out of the District?"

"You're in. I'm out." The tears I had held back flooded my cheeks.

Sharkey gasped, her taut fingers relaxing

on my wrist. Her small eyes widened in disbelief. "But you hate me! Everybody hates me!"

"What's that got to do with it?" I cried. "Who says you have to like everyone? My sister rubs me wrong, but she's still my sister. And you've been plenty hostile. Still, you didn't want to see me hit by lightning, and I don't want to keep you out of the District unless I can prove what I'd like to prove."

Sharkey's nostrils flared. "I've done a lot of lousy things to get ahead, but you gotta believe me, I never put no extra club in your bag. And the reason I want to belong to the District isn't just so I can play them fancy courses or any of that crap. I want to turn pro—the sooner the better—and the District will help. I need a sponsor and when I get one I'm going to move Ma out of the stinking rotten dump we live in—"

"But where's your father?"

"Him!" Sharkey spat out the words. "He cut out the day I was born and it wasn't so long after some punks beat up Ma."

"Oh, Sharkey." I reached out a hand. "I didn't know."

"It's been a great life," Sharkey snorted. "You might say the pits. But maybe starting today it'll get better. I bet you can never guess how I got going on golf."

I shook my head.

"That's the only thing my old man did for me." She bared her teeth. "You might call it my legacy. My old man was a caddy and some member of Maple Hills gave Pa his old set of clubs, and he banged the ball around pretty good when they let the caddies on the course. Well, when Pa did his disappearing act, he left his clubs behind. My first clubs was his clubs." Sharkey's hand flew to her mouth. "I got it! I got it!" Shoving me to one side, she pushed open the door to Bix's office and barged inside, slamming the door behind her.

I stared at the closed door, rocking back and forth on the balls of my feet. Sharkey was in. I was out. Out in the cold. Bix was through with me. Hostile vibes, like an electric current, circulated up and down the dim, damp corridor. If only I were standing on a trapdoor—I'd spring the trap and drop happily into oblivion.

I heard their voices, but no words. His voice was terse. Hers rapid, strident, as if they were arguing. Once I thought I caught the words *eight iron,* but I couldn't be sure. Didn't Sharkey know that there was nothing more to be said on the subject of the missing club? Bix had gone over every possibility time after time after time.

Sharkey, let it be! I cried silently, shaking my fist. Don't you know Bix is in a hurry to get out of here? Every moment precious. What right have you to delay him?

A new sound. Dialing. Bix's voice. I moved closer, anxious to hear. What was going on, anyway? I pressed my ear against the panel. A chair scraped. I jumped back. Whatever had possessed me? Suppose Bix decided to leave. Suppose he burst out the door and found me leaning against it. "Eavesdropping, Kate?" Scorn in his voice, contempt in his eyes. I shuddered. I wouldn't want him to remember me as a busybody. I'd suffered enough humiliation.

I turned my back to the office and walked toward the nearest exit. The voices receded. I held my head high. I didn't need to listen at keyholes. I knew what it was all about. Sharkey was feeling guilty. She was putting on an act to convince Bix of her concern for me.

"Save your breath," I said to the echoing corridor.

15

The exit did not take me to the parking lot as I'd expected. It opened into the golf shop. The storm must have driven all the customers away, for the place was empty. With a feeling of unreality I looked around remembering another night. The merchandise was the same except that now in the height of the season there was more of it. Golf bags in every shade of leather thrust high on the shelves, pull carts on the carpeting, boxes stacked with cleated shoes, racks with golf outfits for men and skirts and tops for women.

My stomach fluttered. How eager I'd been that June night! So hyped up that I'd rushed in here announcing that I wanted to play golf when I had no idea what the game was about. And as things worked out, I did get to play golf—lots of it. Bitterness welled up in me. Why did it have to end up this way?

"Kate?" The voice caught me unawares. I swung around just as Danny was emerging from the storeroom with a load of boxes. He opened the glass case and set the boxes of balls alongside the stacks of gloves. That's how I'd first seen him. Back of the counter. He was the one who had encouraged me.

"Give it a try," he'd said.

I gave it a try. I gave it all I had. But I'd been cheated out of victory.

"I've been waiting to drive you home." Danny slid the glass doors shut. He gave me a close look. "Bix buzzed the intercom when you left his office. That was some time ago."

Should I tell Danny that I'd stood transfixed staring at the office door? Should I tell Danny that I'd been eavesdropping, the sort of low-down trick Mimi would do.

I said nothing.

Danny moved out from behind the counter and put his hands on my shoulders and looked me squarely in the eye.

"This may be the luckiest day of your life. You could have been killed, maimed—"

"I should care."

Danny looked hurt. His grip tightened. "Sorry you didn't make the District. Bix gave me all the details. You know we were all pulling for you, so we feel bad too. And what makes it especially tough is that you lost out to Sharkey. Still," he said, giving me a buck-up pat on the back, "it's hardly the end."

"For me, the end."

Danny chose to ignore that. "Come along, Kate." He opened the front door of the shop and locked it behind him. The rain had stopped. The air smelled fresh and clean. The grass was soggy underfoot, the dry brown spots of yesterday showing flashes of garish green. Birds twittered in the trees, hopped over the fairway and shook their feathers in the puddles.

"Look!" Danny exclaimed, his arm circling my waist and turning to face the west. "A rainbow!"

The rainbow arched in a blaze of color magnificent against the gray backdrop of sky. Fascinated, I watched the spectacle. The sharply defined red-orange rim gradually melded into the blues and greens, and then before my eyes the rainbow faded into nothingness. Just like my golf dreams.

Danny kept right on trying to cheer me up, but it was no go. All the way home I curled up in a cocoon of silence, and at the door I dismissed Danny.

"I'd like to ask you in"—I reached for the knob—"but I'm just too upset."

"Yeah, that I can see." He crossed the threshold right behind me. I would have made a scene and thrown him out, but I was just too tired to be bothered. I staggered into the den and collapsed in the corner of the couch. He sat down beside me and wiped away a tear with his man-sized handkerchief.

"You've got this thing all wrong, Kate," he said gently. "You keep making that stupid statement that it's all over because you didn't make the District."

My throat choked. "All that effort for nothing!"

The strain and struggle of building a sand trap, the hours spent swinging a club, putting, chipping, the afternoons I'd run herd on Cecil and Charles—to come so close to the District only to be shut out by an extra iron that someone had put in my bag.

Danny lifted my chin. "Aren't you overreacting something crazy? Look at it this way. Two months ago you'd never heard of the District."

"Sure. But I still can't help feeling the way I do. No one ever worked harder—"

Danny wouldn't let up. "You didn't know an iron from a wood. Your very first shot struck me right here." Danny tapped his forehead.

My fingertips flew to my temples, just as they had the day my ball slid off my club sideways, blasting his head. How frightened I'd been. I was so sure I had brought on a concussion or worse, and I'd vowed never to play golf again. I smiled just a little. "You know something. I've never shanked since."

"Like they say, you've come a long way, baby."

I had to admit that, but still it would never be the same. "I'm afraid, Danny. With Bix gone and without the challenge of the District, it could very well be downhill all the way."

Danny said, "That's up to you."

I shot back, "You sound just like Bix, lecturing me."

But I knew Danny was right. Who made it to the top? Born winners like Meg Winchester. Then there were the others like Sharkey and

Chipper Daley, who fought their way to stardom, no effort too much. *Never give up.* A rough go all the way. Did I have the stuff champions were made of? Too soon to tell. But I knew one thing about myself: I needed someone to keep me fired up.

Almost as if he'd read my thoughts, Danny said, "I'll be around to help you. And I'm sure Lora—"

"Hey!" a voice called from the porch. "If you're talking about me, at least let me in."

"Coming!" Danny jumped up and unlatched the screen.

Lora stomped down the hall and into the den, her hair bobbing in her barrette. "I'm so mad," she hissed, "I could eat cleats. What a lousy deal, letting Sharkey into the District when everyone knows—"

"Puh-leese!" I put my hands over my ears. "Don't talk about it."

The phone rang, startling me. I reached for the receiver, and when I heard Bix's voice, I cried, "Bix! I thought you'd be long gone by now."

"There's a matter I've been trying to settle for some time, and now—a breakthrough."

"You don't mean—"

"Yes, the missing eight iron."

I gasped.

Bix talked rapidly but I could hear the relief in his voice. "It was Sharkey who put me on the right track," he said. "Like I told you, I checked the clubs of each and every girl who played at Metro that day. What I should have been doing all along was checking out the boys."

"I don't get it."

"This is how it happened. A boy from another park shoved his eight iron in your bag by mistake. A brown bag, like yours. The mix-up occurred on the practice green at Metro. Does this ring a bell?"

My mind did an instant replay and I was mortified. How could I have blanked out that scene on the green? "Oh, Bix, there were some boys chipping and putting and I do remember a lot of golf bags under a tree."

"Case closed," Bix said. "I'm on my way."

"To fame and fortune," I said.

The abrupt voice softened. "Kate, if there's ever a time I can be of help to you—"

"Thanks, Bix. I'll never forget your offer. And we'll be watching you on the tube." Suddenly I knew why Bix had always seemed so familiar to me. At one time or another I'd seen that perfect swing and that granite jaw on the screen.

I cradled the receiver. My eyes darted from Danny to Lora and back again. I could have died. In stops and starts, I told them all I knew.

"It was a mix-up on Metro's practice green. My own fault. My name was called and I left for the tee in such a hurry, I never thought of checking my clubs."

Lora frowned. I dropped my eyes and hurried on. "Some boy goofed. He'd been chipping with his eight iron and he put it in my bag instead of his own." My throat constricted and I could hardly get the words out. "So it wasn't Sharkey after all."

Sharkey. Her name dropped like a stone on my conscience. How close I'd come to keeping her out of the District, damaging her name, ruining her future.

"But, Kate." Lora's face reddened. "I was so sure."

Danny threw back his head and guffawed. "All the best minds, all the best pros, and no one ever thought of checking the right source. But it figures. Tall girl, short boy—the length of the club would be the same."

The screen door slammed and Mimi waltzed

down the hall. She saw us, stopped, and posed prettily in the doorway, her eyes grooving in on Danny. She was wearing a flowered raincoat and a rain helmet with her hair tucked up under it. She took the helmet off and her shining hair cascaded to her shoulders. In a little girl voice she said, "Why, Kate, don't tell me you played golf today?"

"Seventeen holes," I said, "then came the storm. I was almost hit by lightning."

"No wonder you look so tacky!"

"Hey!" Danny said. "She looks plenty okay to me."

Mimi spread her dainty hands and smiled sweetly at Danny. I half expected her to say that she thought his freckles were cute and that his biceps were beautiful, but he stared her down, and after a moment she shrugged and moved down the hall and up the stairs.

Danny lowered his voice. "Jeeps, Kate, how could a gal like you have a sister like that? I bet she couldn't hit a ball fifty yards."

"I'm sure we'll never find out," I said.

Lora gave Danny a jab in the ribs. "Are you crazy, judging a girl on how far she can hit a ball?"

"What else?" Danny said.

I began to laugh. Someone had looked at

Mimi and hadn't seen her golden hair, her pretty face, her darling little ways. It was all too much. A shiver of happiness ran through me.

Lora jumped to her feet. "Let me get you something hot to drink. How about tea?"

I was already reviving, but the tea would only add to my feeling of well-being.

"Great idea," I said.

"Then we can read our fortune in the leaves."

"Really, Lora—"

"Oh, there's something in it all right. Maybe it's because we see what we want to see."

She bustled off toward the kitchen as the phone rang. Ron.

"I'll call Mimi," I said, but he said he didn't want to talk to Mimi—he had something he wanted to say to me.

"I'm busy right now." I could feel Danny's eyes on me.

"No time for your partner?" The voice was low, seductive, but the script sounded out of date, the inflections downright phony. So much had happened. I had barely escaped a lightning bolt. I'd lost out in the District. And my friends were gathered around trying to get me back on the track. I really didn't have time for Ron's type of scenario right now.

"Later," I said, hanging up.

I looked at the phone on its hook and felt a sense of shock. What had I done? Maybe I should call him right back and tell him that I would always—no matter what—have time for my partner. I sat very still, my hands folded in my lap. I waited for my pulse to pound, for my heart to nose-dive like a torn kite. A minute passed, and then another. I felt nothing. Only a sense of relief.

I gave Danny a sidewise glance. "That was Ron," I said at last.

He grinned and I grinned back and we both started to laugh. He moved a little closer to me, but when Lora brought in the tray with the tea cups I pulled back. She set the cups down on the long table in front of us and sat down in the chair opposite.

"Do as I do," she said. She stirred the leaves in her cup vigorously, and when they settled, she peered anxiously at the design.

"Oh," she squealed. "I see golf clubs and a macho man."

"That comes as no surprise," I said.

We both turned to Danny. "What do you see?"

He looked puzzled. "Golf clubs. But some are big and some smaller—ladies' clubs."

Lora blushed and I stirred my leaves round and round.

"What do you see, Kate?" Lora asked.

I sat and stared. Finally I said, "Just tea leaves."

Lora pushed me aside. "You're hopeless, Kate. It's clear as anything. Here, the letters *MS*, and over there, a star. A star means success. You're going to be Ms. Success."

"I'd like that." I put my hands behind my head and closed my eyes and allowed myself to dream. I was sitting behind a mahogany desk and with a stroke of my pen I signed a zillion-dollar oil deal with a tall friendly Texan. He leaned toward me and drawled, "I don't suppose you play golf, honey," and I smiled and said, "I didn't think you were ever going to ask me."

I jerked awake and grabbed my spoon and sent the leaves fluttering into a new design.

"Now what?" Lora's eyes danced with curiosity.

The star and the Texan had vanished. The corporate ladder had collapsed.

"I see a zillion round things," I said.

Lora shook her head knowingly. "Golf balls. You'll never give up your golf."

Funny, I thought, they look like freckles to me.

I laughed. "Conflicting readings. This calls for another tea party. Same people. Same time. Same place. Next year."

"Count on me," Danny said. He moved closer, but this time I didn't pull back.

If you enjoyed this book...

...you will enjoy a *First Love* from Silhouette subscription even more. It will bring you each new title, as soon as it is published every month, delivered right to your door.

Filled with the challenges, excitement and anticipation that make first love oh, so wonderful, *First Love* romances are new and different. Every *First Love* romance is an original novel—never before published—and all written by leading authors.

If you enjoyed this book, treat yourself, or some friend, to a one-year subscription to these romantic originals. We'll ship two NEW $1.75 romances each month, a total of 24 books a year. So send in your coupon now. **There's nothing quite as special as a First Love.**

First Love from Silhouette

NEW BOY IN TOWN
Sixteen-year-old Stacey Hippner loves her parents but she resents their restrictions—especially when they involve Garr Garwin, the new boy in town.

KATE HERSELF
Kate Fleming had always felt the insignificant middle sister. That was before Ross Barrow, the most popular boy in school asked her out.

PLEASE LET ME IN
Melissa Johnson had always dreamed of being in with the most popular crowd. When Greg Scott, hero of the high school football team, begins to date her, she feels she has really made it.

FLOWERS FOR LISA
Lisa Kelly's interest in flowers earns her a summer job at Rick Brewster's father's florist shop. She is thrilled when she and Rick start dating. But she wonders if their relationship will turn out to be only a summer romance.

GIRL IN THE ROUGH
Kate's life as the brainy big sister of adorable, popular Mimi was not easy. When Kate took up golf all this changed.

First Love from Silhouette

THERE'S NOTHING QUITE AS SPECIAL AS A FIRST LOVE.

_____ #1 **NEW BOY IN TOWN** $1.75
     Dorothy Francis

_____ #2 **GIRL IN THE ROUGH** $1.75
     Josephine Wunsch

_____ #3 **PLEASE LET ME IN** $1.75
     Patti Beckman

_____ #4 **SERENADE** $1.75
     Adrienne Marceau

_____ #5 **FLOWERS FOR LISA** $1.75
     Veronica Ladd

_____ #6 **KATE HERSELF** $1.75
     Helen Erskine